a LittLe SoMeThiNG DiffeReNT

a Little SOMeTHiNG DiffeReNT

SANDY HALL

Swoon Reads   New York

A Swoon Reads Book
An imprint of Macmillan Publishers Limited

First published 2014 by Macmillan Children's Books
a division of Macmillan Publishers Limited
20 New Wharf Road, London N1 9RR
Basingstoke and Oxford
Associated companies throughout the world
www.panmacmillan.com

ISBN 978-1-4472-7383-7

1 3 5 7 9 8 6 4 2

A CIP catalogue record for this book is available from
the British Library.

Book design by Ashley Halsey
Printed and bound by CPI Group (UK) Ltd, Croydon CR0 4YY

To all those long-ago afternoons spent at the Hawthorne Library with Mom, Aunt Jude, Matt, Vikki, and Sean

SEPTEMBER

Maribel *(Lea's roommate)*

"I'm going to get us fake IDs," I say to Lea as we walk to class on the first day of school.

"What? That's illegal!" she says.

Even though we've only been roommates for four days, I'm not surprised by her reaction. I think there must be something about the first few days of college that really make people bond together, because I feel like I've known Lea my entire life.

And I can already say unequivocally that she is a great roommate. She's neat, polite, and quiet without being boring.

"Don't think of it as illegal," I say. "Think of it as helping out local business owners."

"You have a skewed perspective of the world, Maribel."

"Drinking is fun!" I say, throwing up my hands. I've only actually been drunk twice in my entire life, once at my sister's wedding and then prom weekend. But still, I know it's fun.

"I don't even really drink!" she says, also throwing up her hands. She's laughing now though.

"Do you want to?" I ask.

"Maybe."

"I mean . . ." I trail off. We're walking onto an enormous green where about half of the academic buildings are located, and I want to take a moment to appreciate the fact that I am actually starting college.

"We're really here," I say, looking around.

"We are," she agrees, smiling. "We should embrace the moment."

"What class are you on your way to?" she asks after a sufficient amount of "embracing the moment" has happened.

"Development of Europe part two." I make sure that my voice is as unenthusiastic as humanly possible.

"I assume that there will be a lot of spoilers if you ever decide to take part one."

"I'll keep that in mind. What are you on your way to?"

"Creative writing."

"How did you get into an awesome upper-level course like creative writing?" I ask as we approach the steps to the English building.

She turns to walk backward for a second and swings right into a very cute guy.

"Oh my gosh," Lea squeaks as she kneels down to help him with his belongings. "I'm so sorry."

"S'okay," he says. He's cute, but super awkward as he tries like four different ways to pick up the books he dropped.

"You're sure?" Lea asks.

He nods but doesn't look at her.

"I just don't want to be late for class on the first day," she says, glancing at me and then back at him.

He settles on the ground and scoops things into his backpack.

He finally looks at her and sort of smiles. "I'm fine."

"Okay, as long as you're okay," Lea says. "See you later, Mar."

I nod and walk toward my own classroom. I think I just got to witness my first collegiate meet cute. I'm sort of assuming meet cutes happen a lot here.

Inga (creative writing professor)

People always expect the first day of school to be crisp and autumnal when the reality is that it's all too often on the hottest freaking day of the year, and the sun burns with the heat of a thousand George Foreman grills.

I stand in front of my latest bunch of creative writing students and look around, trying not to sweat through my thinnest blouse. When I left the house this morning I asked Pam what she thought of my outfit and she said it was like "slutty Little House on the Prairie." I didn't know that was a thing, but I felt proud that I had achieved such a look without even trying.

I hop up on the desk, making sure my Laura Ingalls miniskirt doesn't ride perilously high, and then lean over to check the time on my phone. I'll give them at least four more minutes. It's the first day of school, and even though they're mostly upperclassmen I doubt many of them have been into this far-reaching subbasement before. I swear, it's well below sea level. I would say the depths of hell, but the air-conditioning just kicked in.

There are nineteen seats taken and twenty-seven kids on the roster. I can't help but hope that an odd number of them drop the class. I hate having an odd number of kids in creative writing; it throws everything off when we pair up.

The door opens and my TA comes in.

"Hey, Cole," I say.

"Hey, Inga. Where are we? Twenty thousand leagues under the sea?" he asks, gesturing around confusedly.

"You're telling me. I'm gonna have to leave a trail of Beer Nuts back to my office."

"Why Beer Nuts?"

"Because if I'm wasting food like that it's going to be something I'm not particularly fond of. I would never waste decent nuts."

The door opens again and student number twenty walks in. He's frazzled looking, out of breath, but when he sees us looking at him, he smiles shyly at Cole and me. He takes a seat on the side near the door, next to the angry-looking kid and a girl who looks younger—and more nervous—than the others. He makes blink-and-you'll-miss-it eye contact with the girl before they both blush and turn away.

I glance at the time again and clear my throat. This is the part I'm bad at. I've been teaching my own courses for ten years, but every semester I feel like I mess up my greeting. I always try to be way too cool. I'm thirty-six; what am I trying to prove?

"Hey, hey, hey!" I say, and inwardly groan. I've obviously watched too many reruns of *Fat Albert* in my life. "Let's get this started," I add, clapping my hands.

At least I omitted the word "party" from that sentence this semester. One year I said, "Let's get this party started!" and then ended up on a tangent about how writing can be a party, it can be fun, but there are no kegs involved and limited opportunities to dance.

The students all look up at me attentively, aside from the angry kid. He scratches his ear and rolls his eyes. Guess he's not a *Fat Albert* fan.

"I'm Inga Myerson, and this is Cole . . . my TA." I blank on his last name and mouth "sorry" to him. He shrugs and smiles. "And in case you've trudged into the depths of Narnia by mistake, this is creative writing."

I fall into my usual creative writing spiel and pass out syllabi while I chat. I put it on autopilot and try to pick out the two students who I want to see get together this semester. I have a weird knack for this. It all started when I was a TA for my favorite professor back in grad school. She said she liked to think about the students as stories and enjoyed writing one in her head as class unfolded. I took it one step further and made it a romance.

There were a couple of boys I picked in a seminar in the late nineties who are now happily married with two kids of their own. They're my most successful pairing, but pretty much every semester I see the couples at least get to the point of in-class flirtation.

"I'm going to take attendance, because I like to get everyone's name right eventually. We're going to have to get to know each other in this class, so I hope everyone is comfortable with that idea. There's no way to become writers together without knowing each other at least a little."

The angry kid's name is Victor. I'll remember that.

The nervous-looking girl is Azalea, though she quickly amends it to "Just Lea is fine." She seems less nervous after that.

The last kid who walked in is Gabe. He's got a quietness about him that I like. He has the kind of posture that makes me want to tell him to stand up straight, but I'm sure he has a mother who likes to tell him just that every time she sees him.

There's a girl named Hillary who is everything you imagine a Hillary to be. At least everything I imagined a Hillary to be before Hillary Clinton came on the scene and smashed all of my previous Hillary prejudices, like hair tossing and talking like a Valley girl. This girl is setting that movement back twenty years.

There are other kids, obviously, but these four stick out more than the rest.

When I finish taking roll, I jump back into my spiel.

"I've got a theory," I say.

"That it's a demon," Lea says, so quietly I almost miss it, and I probably would have, but she slaps a surprised hand in front of her mouth. I see Gabe turn to her and smile.

"A dancing demon?" he says quietly.

And then in my finest Rupert Giles impression of all time I say, "No, something isn't right there."

No one else seems to get the joke, but it's in that moment that I know my couple of the semester is going to be Gabe and Lea.

The quick eye contact they shared was good, but the fact that they both picked up on my inadvertent *Buffy the Vampire Slayer* reference makes me feel like they must be kindred spirits. Also it makes me happy to realize that kids these days still watch *Buffy*.

Now I have to figure out a way to orchestrate this relationship.

I hope Cole's into it. I've had TAs in the past who were wet blankets about my little game. I look over at him and he chooses that moment to give me jazz hands and I know we're going to be on the same wavelength.

Bench *(on the green)*

I'm the oldest bench on this green and I get no respect.

I'd like to say there are worthwhile things about the job. And maybe sometimes there are. Sometimes you get a really perfect butt; however, all rear ends are not created equal.

The one currently seated upon me is the kind I appreciate; it's the kind of behind that I would invite back time and again, if I had the ability to speak. And the best part is that it seems to be attached to a person who wants nothing more than to sit. No chatting, no moving around, no graffiti or gum. I could get used to this.

"Gabe," a voice says, sitting next to him. I'm not a big fan of this tuchus. It's ruining the quiet time I was enjoying.

"Sam," the good butt owner says.

"Did you notice that you're sitting like a millimeter away from bird shit?"

"Is there a reason you're here?"

"No. Mom gave me money to buy you lunch on the first day. She was worried about you not eating enough."

"Why would Mom worry about that?"

I imagine there's a meaningful look here and that seems like just enough to make the best butt I've ever known stand up and walk away.

Sam *(Gabe's brother)*

"So, how's your first day back going?" I ask.

He shrugs. My brother has never been much of a talker but in the past nine months he's practically become mute.

"No, seriously, you have to tell me something to tell Mom, or else she's not going to believe me that I took you out for lunch. She's gonna think I kept the money to buy a keg or something."

"Take a picture of me eating," he mutters.

"Or you can tell me something about your day." I pull on his arm to get him to stop and actually look at me. "As your older brother, it is well within my rights to force you to talk."

He sighs. "Fine, tell her that I'm more tired than I expected, but that's what happens when you sit on the couch for nine months. But everything else is going really, really well."

"You're tired?" I prod. Gabe is not a sharer. Gabe is a holder-inner. A holder-inner who is punching me in the arm. "Ow!"

"Why can't she ask me herself?"

"Because she thinks you lie to her."

"Whatever. Why are we still talking about this?"

As we're about to turn off the green, a girl sitting on a bench waves at Gabe and me. Mostly at Gabe, I'd imagine, because I've never seen her before in my life.

He waves back, so I guess it was meant for him.

"Who's that?"

"Just some girl," he says.

"We should invite her to lunch! She's not doing anything." I turn back toward her and he grabs for my backpack to haul me around.

"No we will not."

"You're never gonna get a girl if you ignore them."

"I didn't ignore her."

"I think she's talking to that squirrel."

"She's . . . quirky."

"How do you know her?"

"She's in my creative writing class."

"Oh. Excellent. How was that class?"

He smiles at that. "It was good actually. Aside from the fact that I was almost late because I had no idea there were two levels of basement in the English building."

"Oh, subbasement classes. Yeah, I've been there. They're in many fables, but few have experienced them. I heard there's a clan of mermaids who live in one of the bathrooms."

I'm surprised when Gabe laughs out loud at that. It's really not a great joke to begin with and he hasn't been a big laugh-out-louder recently. He just hasn't been Gabe. I've tried to explain that to our mom, but I don't think she gets it. I think she assumes there's more she could or should be doing, but the secret is that there isn't. This is something Gabe needs to deal with in his own way.

"Anyway, the professor seems cool and the other kids seem okay. It might not be so bad."

As we approach the diner, I want to get one last sentiment out, even though I know he's going to sort of hate me for it.

"You're allowed to talk about it, you know."

He rolls his eyes. "I promise I know."

Squirrel!

I notice the girl eating peanuts. I love nuts.

Nuts, nuts, nuts.

Acorns!

I hop across the grass, trying to be as cute as possible, hoping that maybe if I'm lucky she'll drop one. And her loss will be my gain.

She sees me and smiles.

I'm in! Hooray!

She purposefully drops a peanut on the ground and I eat it up.

Then she drops one on the bench next to her.

Is this a trap?

I take my time eating the first one, watching her, trying to see if she has a net or a cage or a brown bag that she's going to capture me with.

I decide it's all clear, so I hop up on the bench.

She watches two boys walking away across the lawn.

"Do you think they're brothers?" she asks. "They have the same eyes, and maybe the same nose; it's hard to see from here."

I sit up straight. She's talking to me. No one ever talks to me. Oh, how I wish I knew human and could answer her.

Instead I nibble on my peanut.

Victor (creative writing classmate)

I hate everything about this stupid class. We're only a week into the semester and it's already the bane of my existence.

I hate the professor's dumb jokes, I hate the location, I hate the other people in it. In particular, these two idiots who insist on sitting near me every freaking class make me want to stab my own eyes out with my mechanical pencil.

I take a couple of deep breaths. I need to calm down. I need to make it through this semester. This was the only lit class that fit in my schedule; I need it to graduate. I do not want to worry about taking a lit class next semester when I want to be concentrating on my kickass internship.

But seriously, I thought the people in my own major were awful—the comp sci guys can be pretty annoying—but these English majors are the dopiest bunch of assholes this side of the Mississippi. They think they're so deep and filled with meaning. They are not.

And if this dude behind me kicks my chair one more time, I'm not sure what I'm going to do. I know I probably couldn't take him physically, but I would definitely win in a battle of wits.

As I'm thinking that, he kicks it again and I turn to give him a death glare. He sits up straight, moves his freakishly long legs into the aisle, and begins his assault on the chick sitting next to him. Or at least, an assault on her bag. He kicks the shit out of it.

I'm not shocked. He has the biggest feet ever. I suppose they go along well with her abnormally long neck.

Does he realize he would be a lot more effective helping her pick up her bag if he would bend his elbow? He's like Frankenstein's monster over there, all jerky movements and no movable joints.

I tune it out as Big Foot makes random noises of apology

and the Giraffe squeaks that it's not a big deal.

I hate them both so much.

How many days until the semester is over?

Bob (a bus driver)

I have hundreds of kids getting on and off this bus every day. Some kids are real sweethearts and some kids are complete jerks and some kids are neutral. Some are loud in a good way, some in a bad way. There are always a couple who stand out. Sometimes it's because they're just noticeable looks-wise, or sometimes it's a simple case of logistics, like they always get off at a weird stop. My wife, Margie, loves to hear about all of them.

Lately I've been telling her lots of stories about these two kids, a boy and a girl. There's something different about them.

I noticed the boy because he grips the standing bar awkwardly. It's a funny thing how you can be an expert on gripping the standing bar, and this kid is doing it all wrong. He's awkward and it kind of looks like it hurts. I want to give him in a lesson in making it less painful.

And then a couple days ago, I realized that he does it so he can sort of hinge into her personal space every once in a while, because I see him do it even when the bus is almost empty. But he doesn't ever want to get close enough to her to sit near her; it's like he's happy to lurk.

The girl is a different story. I always notice the readers on the bus. I can't read when a bus or car is moving. I get motion sick.

But she's always reading. And he's always holding on like it hurts his arm. And I'm sitting up here thinking about them.

I make the next stop and they get off together, though they don't talk to each other at all. Both of them thank me, and they're the rare kind. Makes me happy, makes me think that maybe they should talk to each other, but I suppose I don't have any control over those things.

I watch them walk until they part ways, her going toward the cluster of dorms, him veering off toward the student center. Then one of them little devils in the back calls out, "Are we going already?"

Some of these kids are just dicks.

Casey (Gabe's friend)

I'm sort-of-almost napping when there's a knock on my bedroom door. I swear to God if it's that new guy from the room off the kitchen again I'm going to go postal on him. I'm not doing anything in my room; I'm napping, there's no way I could be thumping around. He acts like I'm a moose or something up here.

I flip over on my bed and throw myself to the end to open

the door. I have to say the best part of having a tiny room is being able to open the door without getting out of bed. I find Gabe standing on the other side. He's looking straight ahead and makes a confused face when there's no one standing in front of him.

"Hey, man!" I say, sitting up straight and throwing the door open wider for him. He looks down and smiles.

"I couldn't figure out how the door opened," he says, dropping his backpack and taking the computer chair. "I was thinking you rigged it somehow."

"I'm not that kind of engineer," I say.

"What's going on?" he asks.

"Not much. I was napping."

"Oh, damn. I'm sorry, I should have texted. I'll go," he says as he stands up. That's the kind of guy Gabe is. He's always so worried about stepping on other people's toes that he doesn't even notice if you want your toes stepped on. Or like, I don't ever want my toes literally stepped on, but my point is, I like having Gabe around even if he is interrupting my nap.

"No. Sit."

He obeys, because that's also the kind of guy Gabe is. The first time I met him, my freshman year, after I had already been roommates with his brother, Sam, for a couple of months, I was shocked by how different they were. Gabe came to spend a weekend with us to check out the school for himself, and knowing Sam, Gabe was not who I expected.

Where Sam is loud and nearly shameless, Gabe is easygoing and sarcastic. But even with his quieter vibe, it was boring around here without him. I made sure I told him that every time I went to see him last year.

He chews on his thumbnail.

"How's everything going?" I ask, leaning against the wall behind my bed.

"Pretty good. I was just in my creative writing class and there's this girl who has totally . . . captured my attention." He smiles.

"That's cool, but you know that's not really what I was asking." I know he'll talk about everything if and when he wants to, but I like to let him know that I'm around when he's ready.

"No, but that's what I feel like talking about," he says.

"All right, that's fair," I say. "Tell me about this chick."

"She's not a 'chick.'"

"Tell me about this skirt, broad, gal Friday."

"You're the worst, you know?"

"I know."

"She's just in my class and she's cool and I keep thinking I should talk to her because she's always chill about everything in class. Like the other day I knocked her backpack over and instead of giving me a dirty look she was all smiling and telling me it was no big deal."

"What's her name?"

"Lea."

This is weird. Gabe and I don't usually talk about girls. Or I talk about girls and he nods and listens and reprimands me for being kind of a dick about girls. I thought maybe he was asexual or something for a while, but then I realized he was so shy he didn't really know what to do about girls so he kind of ignored them.

"Are you going to talk to her?"

"How do you know I don't already talk to her? Maybe she's outside waiting for me in a pimped-out Lamborghini and we're going to ride off into the sunset."

I raise my eyebrows at him. "You would never buy a Lamborghini. Who even owns Lamborghinis anymore?"

"All right, you caught me," he says, putting his hands up in surrender. "I haven't talked to her. Not really. I kind of mumbled sorry when I kicked her bag, but we haven't exactly conversed."

"You should probably converse."

"Maybe. Could also be fun to like her from afar and make up stories about her in my head and pretend that we're dating."

"So, stalk her?"

"You call it whatever you need to call it," he says with a straight face.

"Listen, I don't want to go all big brother on you," I start.

"By the way, please refrain from mentioning this to my 'big brother,'" he says, using air quotes. "I'd rather not have to deal with Sam about this yet. He'll totally make fun of me. Or worse, he'll tell our mom and she'll start picking out floral arrangements for the wedding."

"Fine, but it'll be tough seeing as I share a room with him."

Gabe stares at Sam's empty bed. "He's not coming back anytime soon, is he?"

"Nah, he has work or something."

"All right, so what's the brotherly advice?"

"Just that she needs to know you exist and that you like her, if you want anything to happen. If you don't want anything to happen, then it doesn't matter. But you probably shouldn't stalk her."

"That's reasonable. Thank you," he says, and then changes the subject.

Maxine (a waitress)

People always ask me, "Maxine, how are you still waitressing at the diner this far into your seventies?" What I tell them is that it keeps me young. What I don't tell them is that I'm already eighty. Working in a college town like this, kids in and out all hours of the night, always hungry, always saying, "Hey, Maxine!" when they see me. I feel like I have a million grandkids without all the trouble of regular kids.

It's a nice, quiet Friday night for coming toward the end of

September. That first month of school always flies by. It's busy, people in and out all the time. But things are calm tonight.

There's a group of girls in one booth, and a group of boys in another. I know some of them, particularly the boys. They're all on the baseball team together, and they can get a bit rowdy at times, but they're good boys, nice manners. They're the kind of boys who girls don't mind being around.

Maybe next time I'll have to accidentally sit them all together. I've done that in the past and it always worked out. But my boss doesn't like it much. Says I can't go messing around, playing with table seatings like that. And to him I say, "Ptooie! This ain't Buckingham Palace!"

Both groups are so polite, which warms my cold heart. Lots of "pleases" and "thank yous." I even get a couple of "ma'ams," which is nearly unheard of these days. Back in my day, it was a pretty standard thing. I had it drilled into me.

But I digress.

I notice two of these cutie pies in particular, because they're making moon eyes at each other every time they don't think anyone's paying attention. And as soon as the other notices, they look away.

It's all so darling I don't know what to do with myself.

So I bring them free pie and hope that's enough to bring them back here again.

Yes, indeed, I hope they come back around here soon.

Danny (Lea's friend)

"What's up, buttercup?" I ask, coming up behind Lea and patting her ass.

"Danno!" she cries, turning around and hugging me long and hard. "I missed you so darn much."

"Why did it take us weeks to have time to get together?"

"I have no idea."

We take a seat on the nearest bench, both carefully avoiding the dried bird crap. We're on our way to meet up with high school friends for dinner, but we have some time to waste before the meetup. Lea and I did a lot of theater together back then and I was thrilled to hear she was going to the same university as me. We've seen each other a few times since I graduated, but it's always pleasant to have a little Lea time.

"So, how's life?"

"Good," she says, smiling wide.

"You look like eighty-five million dollars," I tell her.

"This old thing?" she asks, swishing around the cardigan she got on super sale with me at Old Navy last winter.

I laugh.

"How about you? How's the life of an upperclassman?" she asks.

"Good. I don't know that junior year is going to be much different than all the other years. You know, new semester, new classes, all that crap," I say, letting my eyes roam. "Oh my God!" I yell, clutching her arm.

"What is it? A bug? A rat? A cockroach?"

"No," I whisper, leaning close. "The boy of my dreams." I take her head and turn her in the direction he's walking.

"Gabe Cabrera is the boy of your dreams?" she asks.

"Oh, totally. He's amazing. One of my housemates lived on the same floor as him freshman year and sometimes we end up at similar gatherings. One time he totally flirted with me," I brag.

"Wow."

"He's so charming and one of those like sneak-attack gay guys. Like you don't know he's gay and then he sneaks up on you, and GAY!"

"I didn't know he was gay."

"Oh, for sure," I tell her. "One time he complimented my jeans."

She looks like she's taking this fact in. "In addition to the time he flirted with you?"

"Yes, I'm very lucky."

"You obviously are."

"Come on," I say, pulling her up.

"But we're meeting people . . ." she says, pointing in the opposite direction.

"And we will, but first we should stalk Gabe for a little while. We have at least twenty minutes until we need to be at the restaurant."

"All right, let's do it."

He hasn't gotten very far, just barely onto the sidewalk that leads off the green toward the other end of campus.

"Tell me about Gabe," she says as we walk. "He's in my creative writing class."

"Creative writing, be still my heart," I say.

"Cute, right?" She threads her arm through mine and leans in closer.

"Totally. I thought he was majoring in something else, like teaching phys ed or something. And he's on the baseball team, or maybe he was on the baseball team? Anyway. I used to see him around all the time and then last semester he disappeared, fell right off the face of the Earth, so I haven't seen him in almost a year. I was starting to worry that he graduated or transferred or flunked out."

"Don't talk so loud," she mumbles. "I think he can hear you."

She's right, I should be more discreet. "I get so darn excited about him though. He's like this perfect mystery boy to me."

"He's a perfect mystery boy to almost everyone."

"He is. I think I like to keep him that way. That's gotta be the only reason I have yet to make a proper approach."

She nods in understanding.

"I can't believe I haven't asked you," I say, loathe to change the subject, but aware that I need to bring this up before I forget. "How's the roommate?"

"She's good! Her name is Maribel. She's really funny but not in a mean way. She has incredible hair. I just want to touch it all the time."

"You have nice hair," I say, batting at her short, straight bob.

"Not like Maribel."

"We'll see about that."

"She wants to get us fake IDs." Lea crinkles up her nose at the thought.

"That's a great idea. Then you can come out with me all the time! Or at least, you could when I finally turn twenty-one next month."

"You don't have a fake?"

I shrug. "It didn't seem worth it. Most clubs are eighteen and up, and I don't mind not drinking. And with an October birthday I'm the oldest of all my friends anyway."

She smiles.

"Now, getting back to the matter at hand, no one really knows where Gabe was all that time. I'm sure that his friends do, but I like to imagine that he was overseas or taking care of a dying relative or something romantic like that."

"Isn't this basically the plot to *10 Things I Hate About You*?"

"Rest in peace, Heath," I say automatically. "But yeah. It's probably something dull like his parents didn't have enough money, or he briefly transferred somewhere else and hated it."

"We should pretend that he was overseas."

I think about that. "But if he went abroad it wouldn't have been a secret."

"How do you know it was a secret as opposed to something you personally just don't know?"

"Well, my housemate Maureen, you'll meet her; she's the one who lived on the same floor as him, and while they didn't all keep in close touch, she knows people who still know him and are friends with him, but they were always vague about where he was."

Lea looks doubtful. "So people would come out and ask his friends directly where he was and they wouldn't answer?"

"Well, I don't know if Mo-Mo ever asked directly. But I guess so?"

"Maybe he was in rehab," she says.

"He doesn't strike me as the kind of person who does drugs. Although, if he was on the baseball team maybe he was on steroids or something."

"Or maybe it was for painkillers. Or NyQuil."

"You can't go to rehab for NyQuil."

"You do realize that sometimes you're no fun to joke around with and you take my silliness far too seriously."

I throw my head back and laugh.

"Maybe it was crystal meth. Or sex addiction!" I say in a dramatic whisper.

"I mean, really, Dan. If he's half the man of mystery that you claim he is, he was probably working abroad as a tattoo artist for the queen of England or something."

"Which begs the question, what kind of tattoo would the queen of England get?"

"A corgi in a crown," she says, not missing a beat. "What kind of tattoo would Gabe get?"

He's several blocks away from us now; we've been walking at a slothlike pace and need to take the next turn, but we can still see his red T-shirt in the distance.

"A 'Mom' tattoo," I say with a grin.

"Definitely, on his bicep."

"Totally."

"You're sure he's gay?" she asks, making a sad little face.

"I'm pretty sure," I say, scratching my head. "I mean, my gaydar could be on the fritz, but that doesn't happen often."

She smiles. "Well then, our mission will be to get you guys together. And to find out what his mysterious disappearance was about last semester."

"Yes, agreed." I extend my hand to shake with her to seal the deal. Then we head over to dollar tacos at Casa del Sol.

Pam (Inga's wife)

"Now that we're a few weeks into classes, I have to know, who is your couple of the semester?" I ask as we sit down to dinner Friday night. It's rare that we both sit down at the table to eat, but if it happens it's going to happen on a Friday night.

"I can't believe I haven't told you," Inga says, her eyes lighting up. "They're a boy and a girl this time, Gabe and Lea. When I tell you they're adorable, I mean they are adorable."

"That's what you say about all of them," I say, leaning back and sipping my wine.

She rolls her eyes. "They are all adorable, but there's something special about these two. I feel like I would have picked them out anywhere, not just in class."

"I've heard you say that before."

"I know! But they've been giving me some great material. She read a short assignment in class the other day and I think he definitely drooled."

"Maybe he just got back from the dentist."

"Why do you insist on teasing me?" she asks, glaring at me. "They have a story. I'm telling you, there's no way they don't have a story. They have this chemistry that's impossible to ignore. I don't even know what it is. But I'm going to do whatever I can to get them together."

I shake my head even though I can't help but smile. My girl has a passion for matchmaking.

"Or to at least talk to each other."

"At the very least," I agree, teasing her. She doesn't even notice and just keeps on going.

"They sit next to each other almost every class. Or

sometimes Victor sits between them," she says, making a face.

"Curse you, Victor!" I say, thrusting my fist in the air. "Who's Victor?"

"He's one of those kids who have to take the class for a requirement."

"Oh, one of those."

"He had the balls to come see me at office hours and request that I change something on the syllabus because of his own personal timetable. I wanted to smack him."

"There's always one."

"He kind of reminds me of that Indian kid from Mean Girls. . . ."

"Kevin G.," I say without missing a beat.

"Yes! Except scarier, because this kid is not happy about being in this class. I'm a little bit worried he's going to set something on fire. He's like a cesspool in the midst of my creative writing oasis."

"I know the type."

"Anyway, sometimes they do that thing. Where one of them looks over at the other like they're going to say something and then looks away just as the other senses someone's looking at them so they look up."

"Ugh, the bad timing thing."

"It's the worst. But Gabe and Lea will fall in love, mark my words," she says, tapping her finger on the table to punctuate her statement.

"These words, they are marked."

We're quiet while we eat for a few minutes.

"So what's new in the world of astrophysics?" she asks.

"We've been married for five years and you still have no real concept of what I do with my days."

"No, I really don't."

OCTOBER

Charlotte (a barista)

Getting stuck with this God-awful morning shift all by my-self is basically the worst thing that has ever happened in the history of my career at Starbucks. It's this new manager, she doesn't seem to understand that I have to always work with Tabitha or Keith. They keep me level and they keep me from wanting to strangle customers.

And look who just happens to walk in—Gabe the loser. It's an interesting and terrible phenomenon about working at Starbucks, you really do get to know the regulars' names. And unfortunately they get to know yours. Gabe's been com-ing in for a long time, though he wasn't around much last year. I almost missed him, but now he's come back, flakier than ever. He's even talking to himself right now.

Tabitha and Keith like to pretend that Gabe is some kind of special snowflake. That he's the cutest, shyest, most wonderful boy on the planet. Personally, I think they're nuts. I think the kid is straight-up loopy and in the worst way possible.

"Hi," I say as Gabe gets to the register, trying to put on my best Starbucks smile and failing.

He says nothing, continuing to stare at his shoes.

"Hello!"

Nothing.

"Yo! Dude!" I glance around the register to find something to flick at him.

The girl behind him nudges him and Gabe looks up.

"Sorry," he mumbles.

"S'okay," I say, even though I really don't mean it.

"What can I get for you?"

"Grande coffee, room for milk."

"Sumatra or Pike Place?" Normally I would assume Pike Place, but Gabe mixes it up sometimes.

He stares at me like I'm speaking a foreign language even though it's a fairly basic and obvious question.

"Sumatra or Pike Place?" I'm practically yelling. It's ridiculous.

He stares at my lips and does a weird combination of a

shake and shrug. "I don't know what you're saying."

I point at the urns behind me that say "Sumatra" and "Pike Place."

"Oh, Sumatra's fine," he says. I feel a little bad; his cheeks are a burning red that you usually only find on cinnamon candies and he's blinking a lot as he hands me a gift card.

For the life of me I can't figure out why Tabitha has such a gigantic crush on him. She could do better, I think as I hand him his drink.

"Thanks," he mumbles, digging deep into his pockets and dropping a few coins in the tip jar. I have to fight the urge to thank him profusely for his seven-cent tip. Wait until I tell Tabitha and Keith how weird he was today.

Victor (creative writing classmate)

I don't understand what kind of horrors I must have committed in a past life that I'm being forced to endure this kind of punishment in the present.

Why do Big Foot and the Giraffe always sit by me? I swear I randomize my seat each class and somehow I still end up between or near these two dillweeds every single time. There's nothing about me that's inviting, I'm sure of it.

I'm tired of playing chaperone to their weirdo mating ritual. Talk to each other already! You're in college! Stop being coy and adorable. And I don't mean adorable in a positive way.

They're cloying and maybe even a little bit pathetic.

I wonder what Big Foot would do if I asked her on a date in front of him. Maybe he would stomp on me with one or both of his feet.

"Victor?" I'm roused out of my thoughts by Inga. She thinks she's so cool in her hipster glasses and tiny cardigans and her spiky blond hair.

"Yes?"

"It's your turn to share your story idea."

I need to start thinking of new and creative ways to get out of this class. That's what my story idea should be.

Inga (creative writing professor)

As one of the other students leaves office hours, I'm delighted to find Gabe and Lea waiting for me in the hallway. In fact, when they look up as the door opens, I go so far as to hold up a "wait one second" finger, just to make them hang out alone together a little longer.

I close the door and drum my fingers on my desk, straining my ears in case they decide to talk to each other.

I count to thirty.

I'm aware of how unprofessional this is and yet I can't stop myself.

I count to thirty again.

Still not a word from the hallway. I sigh and open the door.

"Who's next?" I ask, all too aware of how overly bright my smile is.

"Ladies first," Gabe says. And it's like all three of us are surprised for a second by his chivalry. He awkwardly leans against the wall and looks in the other direction.

"All right, Lea," I say. "Come on in."

We chat for a few minutes. I tell her how impressed I was with the direction she took on the most recent short-story prompt.

She sits up straighter and smiles at the compliment.

"Thank you, I wasn't sure how the assignment would come out. I feel a little . . . young sometimes in there, quite frankly."

"You're a first-year?"

"Yes."

"I have had many first-years who are far better writers than the upperclassmen. I don't think age has much to do with writing. I think it's something that can certainly improve in time, but there's no age limit on how old you need to be to write well."

"I feel better hearing you say that."

"Have you made any friends in the class?" I ask, prodding, probably getting too close to my personal interests.

She scrunches her nose and peers at the door. "Not really. There's that guy, Gabe, he's nice, but I don't know that he's looking for a friend."

I nod and smile and keep my lips closed tight so that I don't burst out with something seriously inappropriate like, "I knew it!"

I take a deep breath. "Well, it's good to find critique partners. We'll be talking about that more soon."

"All right," she says, standing up.

"Is that all? You didn't need anything specific?"

"No, mostly I just wanted to make sure I was on point with everything and you cleared that up pretty quickly. So, thanks."

"Excellent." Then I have a bit of a lightbulb moment. "Can you send Gabe in?" Now she has no choice but to talk to him.

She opens the door and gestures for him to come in without saying a word. I suppose at least she smiles at him. These two and their nonloquacious natures are going to be the death of me.

He scrambles into the seat across from me and dives right in without so much as a greeting, like he's been rehearsing these words over and over again. Like if he doesn't get them out he might just explode.

"I've been having trouble with writing too many words," he explains quickly, wiping his hands on his jeans.

"That's not necessarily a problem," I say, my words slow, hoping to calm him down a bit.

"Even for these more limited short stories?"

"I mean, try not to write five thousand words for a

two-thousand-word assignment, but if you want, bring this one in and we'll work on phrasing together," I offer. "It's amazing how many writers could chop down their word count by using more precise vocabulary or getting rid of unnecessary descriptors."

He smiles and nods.

"Any other questions?"

"It's not so much a question. It's more like a concern. I'm going to have to read an assignment in front of the class, right?"

"Yes. More than one, probably."

"There's no getting out of that?"

I smile sympathetically, but shake my head.

"I feel like I'm going to end up editing myself a lot, because, I don't know, the idea of sharing some of this stuff with strangers makes me feel . . ."

"Vulnerable?" I suggest. I get this concern a lot.

"Yeah," he says with a sigh, his ears turning red.

"That's a little tougher. I'm not going to tell you to ignore the way you're feeling or try to forget it, but writing about something that makes you feel emotional isn't necessary for this course. If you find that the idea of presenting something you've written is out of the question, come see Cole or me, and we'll be happy to help you out without you losing any points."

"All right," he says, nodding.

"Is that all?"

"Yes."

"Jeez, you kids are making life easier and easier these days."

"I could make something up?"

"Nah, I'll just get home earlier than usual."

"Thanks for your help," he says, standing, smiling, and slipping out the door.

I sit back in my office chair and spin around. It's not much, but I think there was at least a tiny bit of progress made today.

Sam (Gabe's brother)

The girl Gabe knows from creative writing is wandering around the library stacks looking increasingly lost. To be more specific, it's the girl Gabe has a *crush* on from creative writing.

"Hey," I say, approaching her when I see her for the third or fourth time.

"Hi," she breathes, looking from me to the shelf label and back again.

"Do you need help?"

"Do you work here?"

"Yes."

"Oh, then sure, maybe you can help me."

She shows me the slip of paper she's holding.

"You're one level too high," I say. I push the cart of books

I'm supposed to be shelving out of the way and I lead her down the back staircase to the floor below us, bringing her to the right section.

"Thank you so much," she says, sliding the book off the shelf and hugging it to her.

"No problem. I'm Sam," I say, extending my hand to shake.

"Lea," she says. She has a decent grip. I'm impressed.

"You know my brother, Gabe, don't you?"

She looks back up at me from the book. "What? No. I mean . . ." She pauses, obviously flustered. She and Gabe would seriously be a match made in heaven. "We have a class together, but I don't know him. Not, I don't *know him* know him. We don't . . . we aren't friends."

I nod and try not to smile too much, even though I'm holding back a laugh. "I'll tell him you said that."

"No!" she says.

"I was joking," I promise, putting a hand on her arm.

"Thanks again," she says, holding up the book and backing away.

I watch her walk away and spend the rest of my shift trying to think of scenarios to get those two crazy kids together. At least it makes the hours move faster.

———————

Squirrel!

The best part of this time of year is all the acorns. Acorns are delicious and amazing and the best thing that anyone could ever eat. If you're not eating acorns you are seriously missing out. I tell all my friends about the amazingness of acorns and sometimes they just stare at me like I'm crazy. But I'm only crazy for acorns.

I see a boy and a girl. The girl gave me peanuts once and she always looks at the boy a lot. He looks at her too. But they always look at each other at the wrong second. But today they look at each other at the right second and they both smile so wide it looks like they're laughing.

I hope they're laughing.

I hope they like acorns. Maybe I'll throw some acorns at them. No, that's a bad idea. I don't want to lose my acorns. I don't want to share. Call me a bad squirrel, but I do not like to share my acorns.

Maybe that makes me a good squirrel. The consummate squirrel. The very definition of a squirrel.

Hillary (creative writing classmate)

"We're going to be starting on our first long-term critiquing assignment," Call-me-Inga declares one rainy October day. She says it like she is so thrilled, like it's the best thing to happen since movable type was invented or whatever

English professors get excited about.

"We're going to be doing a series of simple stories, a thousand words give or take, and then sharing them with a partner over the next few weeks. It will give you both a chance to see firsthand how someone else works on these assignments, and then we'll switch around. I think it's important that we all learn from each other."

I sit up straight and raise my hand, not bothering to be called on before speaking. "What topics will we be writing about?"

"I think something simple like a particular childhood memory that stands out to you would be a good place to start. It can be sad, happy, funny, but get it to a thousand words. It doesn't have to be extremely personal. If you feel like this topic might tap into something like that, come see me in office hours. You don't have to give any specifics, but we can work something out."

Truth be told, that's part of what I respect about Call-me-Inga, even if she can be sort of a tool. She's realistic about limitations people might have when it comes to topics. Like what if I was abused as a kid and everything about my childhood makes me think of that? Although I feel like if you're having those kinds of problems you're probably not in college taking creative writing. You're probably like in prison making toilet wine.

These are the kinds of thoughts I really need to keep to myself.

I probably don't want to think too hard about toilet wine, either. One time my roommate and I made a huge tub of punch in a Rubbermaid storage bin and used grape Kool-Aid and all the guys said it looked like toilet wine. But how would frat boys even know what toilet wine looks like?

"Was there something else?" Call-me-Inga asks me. I must have zoned out thinking about toilet wine.

"We can pick partners?"

"Of course. This isn't kindergarten." She smiles like she said something super clever and I go back to disliking her even if I do respect her.

I run my hands through my hair and look around at the class. There are an even number of kids so that's good news. But I don't want to get stuck with that snoozefest Victor. I've had my eye on cutie pie Gabe all semester, so I lean across the empty chair in between us. He kind of looks like this guy my sister dated who drove a motorcycle. He was hot. She was too stupid to hang on to him though.

"Gabe!" I say, like we're old friends.

He doesn't respond. I ball up a piece of paper and throw it at him. He jumps and looks over at me. I toss off my most seductive "come be my creative writing partner" finger wave.

He raises his eyebrows.

"We should work together," I say, leaning my hand on my chin. I'm almost annoyed at myself for using all my best stuff on this semi-loser in class, but he's not really a semi-loser.

He's particularly cute when he doesn't shave and he gets all flustered when he has to talk to the class. If only he would wear cooler shoes. Maybe while we work together on this assignment I can coach him on different footwear. They're always slip-ons, never anything with laces. And they're always kind of cheap looking. At least they're not Crocs.

"So?" I prod.

"Oh." He glances away. "Um, I guess." He turns to me and nods.

Score.

We drag our chairs together.

"Before we start, I have to ask. Are you Italian? I love Italian guys."

"Um. I'm mostly Portuguese and Welsh."

"South American, even better."

He gives me a weird look. "You do know that Portugal isn't in South America, right?"

"Of course, silly," I say, touching his arm. "I was joking!"

Where the eff is Portugal?

Inga (creative writing professor)

I finish giving the assignment and I watch as Lea makes a note and Gabe stares at the back of her head. It's perfect timing for them to finally become friends. I hope neither of them had a painful childhood. I find that this is the best assignment to get my couple of the semester to really engage with each other. There's something about having to share childhood memories that always brings people closer.

And time is ticking for Gabe and Lea. I haven't even seen them talk to each other yet. They spend plenty of time staring dreamily at each other, so there's obviously an attraction there. It's like they've formed a covert mutual-admiration society, and now it's time for them to share it with each other.

Lea looks up from her notebook and smiles at me. But then we both notice at the same moment that Gabe is talking to Hillary.

Dammit, Hillary! You are cordially uninvited from the covert mutual-admiration society. It's like I can see all of my hopes and dreams of Gabe and Lea falling in love go out the window with each toss of Hillary's long overly highlighted mousy brown hair. I know that it's mouse brown under those expensive shades of ash and honey. Not that I think Gabe is the kind of boy who's particularly susceptible to hair tossing, but I don't know him very well and therefore cannot give him the benefit of the doubt.

I sigh so loudly that I feel like half the first row notices, so instead of actually wringing Hillary's neck I smile and turn away for a moment, regaining my composure. Pam is going to hate hearing about this. In part because it emphasizes how emotionally invested I am in this nonrelationship.

I turn back to check on Lea and she looks okay. The girl who was sitting on the other side of her seems to be engaging her. But I wanted Gabe and Lea to fall in love while talking about his tenth birthday party, or her using the quilt her grandmother made her to build the world's best blanket fort. Or that time that Lea got her head stuck in between the rungs of a chair and Gabe fell off a roof because his older sister told him that he'd be able to fly. These are the kinds of stories that bond people together. These are all examples of actual essays that students have written in the past.

Now that's never going to happen because of Hillary's existence.

I didn't know I could hate the name Hillary quite this much. I am seething with almost as much rage as Victor experiences in this classroom on a daily basis.

I look at Lea sympathetically and she smiles back, her usual smile. This is not over though between Hillary and me. She has poked the bear.

Sam (Gabe's brother)

I'm about to leave the student center when I notice Gabe hiding in the corner in the back, almost out of sight behind the stairs. Our mom keeps bugging me to keep an eye on him, even though I keep telling her that he's fine.

I sit down opposite him. "I didn't even realize there were seats back here."

He doesn't seem to notice, so I knock on the table and he startles, pulling out his earbuds and looking over at me.

"Hey," he says. "I didn't hear you."

"Shocker. I was just saying that I didn't even know there were seats back here."

He looks around like he had no idea where he was sitting. "I think they must have added them recently. I like it though. Out of the way."

I nod. "How's it going?"

"All right."

"What are you up to?"

"I'm supposed to meet up with my creative writing critique partner."

"Are you working with that chick Lea?"

"Nah, with the most annoying girl in the world. I wish it was Lea." And from the face he's making I believe him. Unfortunately, the older brother in me rears its ugly head.

"So you do like her!"

He rolls his eyes.

"Have you talked to her yet?"

"No."

"I talked to her the other day."

That gets his attention. "What? What did you say to her, Sam?"

"Nothing, I swear!" I hold up my hands in surrender.

He glares at me. "You promise you weren't an ass?"

"Promise."

"I don't believe you."

"Fine."

"Fine."

We've come to a stalemate, but I decide to proceed anyway.

"You should talk to her. She's nice."

He shrugs.

"Come on, man, why not?"

"You know why," he says. And I do know why, but it seems to me that all of his issues are kind of dumb, and I'm allowed to think that because I'm his brother. "Let's talk about something else, anything else."

"How's the life of an academic residence mentor, or whatever word-salad title you have?"

"It's not easy. I had this girl come see me crying the other night about her calc class. I've never taken calc; precalc was more than enough for me. So I kind of had no advice to give her."

"That's tough."

"It is. I feel bad for the kids because they kind of got me by default, you know? If I hadn't lost my scholarship they would have someone more useful."

"I'm pretty sure the school wouldn't have given you this title if they thought you were useless."

"And I'm pretty sure the school gave me the position because they felt bad for me."

"But still," I say, trying to grasp for something, anything, to pull him out of this spiral of self-pity that I can sense brewing. "You have a single."

He chuckles at that. "Very true."

"Having a single sounds kind of amazing."

He looks at me with his eyebrows raised.

"It's been a long three years of Casey farting in his sleep."

Gabe laughs at that.

"Want to give me a swipe to the dining hall?" I ask, realizing that I haven't eaten in like a thousand years and that I have no food in my house.

"Nah, I have to meet up with the most annoying girl in the world, remember?"

"Oh, that's right. How did you get stuck with the most annoying girl in the world?"

He wrinkles his nose. "She asked me to work with her and I had no idea how to say no. I was so shocked that it wasn't Lea asking that I fell into some kind of fugue state."

"Why is she so annoying?"

"Well, for starters, she thinks Portugal is in South America."

I shake my head and laugh.

"That's tough, dude," I say.

"Life is tough sometimes," he says, like a wise old man.

"It is, but—" I stop myself. I look at him, at the way he has books spread all over the table and the crease of concentration in his forehead. "It doesn't have to be as hard as you make it. And I know you hate when I say it and I might just be . . . pissing into the wind and I don't want to start a fight, but you could like, let other people help you with stuff sometimes."

He stares at me and for a second I think he might cry.

"I know," he says finally.

"Good, as long as you know."

"I really do. That's why I started seeing a therapist."

"Good for you," I say, a little surprised. But I knew that my parents had been encouraging him to do just that. Before we can make this a Hallmark moment, I catch sight of a girl whose smile is so broad it has to be fake.

"I'm going to guess that's your partner," I say, gesturing with my chin.

"Yes," he says, shoulders deflating. "Unfortunately."

I rush out of there then with just a quick wave over my shoulder. I'm not in the mood to meet the most annoying girl on earth.

Frank (Chinese-food delivery guy)

These orders can't be right. They're exactly the same items for two different people in two different dorm rooms in the same building. We have to stop letting Lin answer the phone, she can never keep these things straight. She definitely can't be in charge on Sunday nights anymore, that's for sure.

I call both rooms anyway. Maybe the one whose order is wrong will take it, or at least they'll know I'm here and they weren't ignored. I hate having to turn around and go back to the restaurant, but I suppose it's all part of the job.

I wait for what seems like a million years, hanging out in the lobby, trying not to look like I'm casing the joint. My phone is blowing up. Seems like everyone wants to go out tonight for some reason, but I have lab at 9 a.m. and there's no way I'm messing with that. I have an A in that class and I don't want to lose it.

Finally both elevators slide open, and a girl emerges from one and a guy from the other.

"Delivery?" I say, holding up the bags.

They both walk over, glancing at each other.

"Is it possible you guys ordered the same thing?"

"Sesame noodles with chicken and a side of fried dumplings?" the girl says, looking from me to the kid.

"Yeah," the kid says, so quietly that it's like barely a word and more of an exhale.

"Seriously?" I ask.

He nods and she smiles.

"And you're not together?" I ask, confused. "This has never happened before. It might not seem like a big deal, but I've been delivering for my family's restaurant for six years and it's literally never happened before."

"No," the girl says. Guess she's the spokesperson tonight. "Not together. But glad we could break some kind of statistical record for you."

"Cool. Cause I was gonna say you could have ordered the bigger size of dumplings for less money and more dumplings."

They both smile at that. "More dumplings are never a bad thing," the girl says.

I hand them their orders and they pay, both of them pretty decent tippers. As I walk out, I look over my shoulder and they're staring at each other while they wait for the elevator.

Maribel (Lea's roommate)

Lea practically attacks me as I walk through the door Sunday night after spending the weekend at home.

"I missed you, too," I say, my hands full of Lea and clean laundry.

"The worst thing happened," she wails.

"What? Oh my God. What happened?" I steel myself for

awful news. I try to run through my head what could possibly be this bad.

"Gabe lives here!"

"Isn't that a good thing?"

"Well, yes, but I didn't know he lived here. All this time! How did I not notice? We always get off at the same bus stop. But I never even thought he lived in this building. I just figured he lived in the general area."

"You realize this isn't awful? Close proximity to a crush is not a bad thing."

"That isn't the awful thing."

I sigh, dumping my laundry on the bed. She throws herself on her bed while I start putting things away.

"Tell me your troubles," I say.

"So, I ordered Chinese," she starts.

"Did you save me any?"

"There are some leftover dumplings in the minifridge."

"Yummy."

She rolls her eyes. "When the delivery guy gets here he buzzes me down, and lo and behold when I get to the lobby, who steps out of the other elevator but Gabe in the flesh."

"Amazing."

"I thought so, too," she agrees. "Of course he doesn't say anything the whole time the delivery guy is babbling about how we ordered the same exact food and how that never happens. And then the guy asks if we're together, which is just a little bit embarrassing."

I make a "so-so" gesture with my hand.

"But then it got way worse."

"How?"

"We were waiting for the elevator together and kind of looking at each other, or at least glancing over at each other at regular intervals. And I was trying to think of some topic of conversation. . . ."

"You should have told him how much you liked the essay you critiqued of his in class last week."

"Yes, that is something a normal person would have said."

"Oh no. What did the non-normal person say?"

"Well, this idiot looks him in the eye and says, 'As a Chinese person, I can tell you that you have great taste in Chinese food.'"

"That could be worse," I say.

"Would you ever in a million years tell someone that you felt as a Mexican person that they have great taste in Mexican food?"

"Well . . . when you put it that way . . ."

She pulls the hood of her sweatshirt up and tightens the strings so only her nose pokes out.

"Lea, I'm teasing. It's really not that bad," I say, sitting next to her on the bed. "What did he say back?"

She loosens her hood so she can speak. "He just kind of

stood there, opening and closing his mouth at me."

"I mean, it would have been better if you had complimented his essay, but I don't think all is lost just because you said something mildly weird to him."

"The first time I finally get up the nerve to talk to him and that's what I say? I don't talk like that. That's not something I would say."

"You should have complimented his essay and then invited him to eat with you."

"Why aren't you always around to coach me in these moments? Why do you leave me floundering alone in the world?"

"I don't have answers for these questions."

She squints into the distance. "To be fair, had I asked him up to eat with me, I know it would have been a disaster. There's no way I could have been cool around him. I would have ended up talking about my family tree or how the plural of 'cul-de-sac' is 'culs-de-sac.'"

"Maybe he would have appreciated that," I say, rubbing her back.

"I just have to keep reminding myself that I'm not actually blowing my chances. I don't have to be super cool around him."

"Keep telling yourself that."

She tightens her hood back up and shakes her head.

———————

Charlotte (a barista)

"Have you seen my perfect honeybunch Gabe lately?" Tabitha asks during a quiet moment. She obviously wants to gossip, and while I don't want to work, I'm not sure if I'm in the mood to talk about Gabe. "I've seen him a couple of times, but not nearly enough, so I thought I could live vicariously through you. If you've seen him."

"You are babbling."

"He's just so cute!"

"I think he has something wrong with him," I say. I don't want to be too mean about him, mostly because Tabitha is a kind person. You don't meet kind people like Tabitha all the time and definitely not working at a place like Starbucks. But I don't want her to get her hopes up.

"No way! He's adorable."

"He was in here a couple of weeks ago and he was so out of it that I think he was seriously stoned."

She shrugs. "I'm not one to judge people's drug habits."

"It was ten a.m."

"Maybe he was sleepy."

"I had to ask him about forty times what size coffee he wanted."

"You mumble."

"Every single time he comes in here, he has trouble answering the simplest questions. The time before that it was

♥ 55 ♥

Sumatra or Pike Place, the time before that it was whether he wanted his pastry warmed up. I should stop asking questions."

"He's just quiet. The past few times I've seen him in here, it's been around the same time as this girl Lea. And they're always so shy when they see each other and almost sort of smile. It's like we're getting to watch their love unfold before us."

"You've been spending too much time with your cats lately."

"You've been spending too much time with your head up your ass lately," she shoots back.

I make a shocked face and throw the steam wand rag at her.

"Gross," she says. "I don't want your dried milk rag in my face."

"I don't want you waxing poetic about love between a stoner and some random chick in my face."

"I totally ship them," Tabby says, leaning her hand in her chin and staring at the door, like she's willing them to come in together.

"I shouldn't even ask," I mutter.

"Like when you want characters on a TV show to get together. And you 'ship' them, you want them to be in a relationship and to live happily ever after."

"I thought you shipped him with yourself."

"Well, obviously, in an ideal world. He's into Lea though, I can tell. So if we can't find happiness together, I definitely want him to find happiness with her."

"Okay, Tab, tell me honestly. Have you been writing

fanfiction about Starbucks customers?" She throws the rag back at me as the bell on the door jingles and we both turn to look. It's not Gabe or Lea.

"Maybe I should," she says with a smile.

I roll my eyes.

"I just like them. I like how he looks at her and I like how she looks at him. I think they would have beautiful babies."

"Oh, Tab," I say, shaking my head.

"I like the idea that we're getting to watch their lives without them knowing. And I know that might sound voyeuristic and weird and pathetic, but it also makes me happy. And I don't have a ton of that kind of happy in my life at the moment, so let me enjoy some damn Starbucks customers falling in love!"

"I hate to have to be the one to tell you this," I say. "But I saw him in here yesterday with some chick with super-fake-looking highlights."

"And you're only telling me this now!"

"I only just remembered!"

"Well, that's predictable," she says, her face falling.

"Maybe it's not what we think it is! Maybe they're related," I say. I honestly have no idea why I'm defending that dork.

It gets busy after that and we lose track of the conversation, but I have to admit I think about Gabe and Lea on and off for the rest of the day.

Danny *(Lea's friend)*

I see her walking down the street away from the bus stop with a few of her friends. It's Halloween, so I almost didn't recognize her with her hair all teased and crimped.

"Azalea!" I call, and trot across the street.

"Danny!" she cries, throwing her hands up and doing a little jig.

"You are totally eighties," I say.

"I totally am!"

"You are D-R-U-N-K!"

"Just a little; we pregamed," she says, nodding. "Maribel promised it would be fun and it is fun!"

"Hi, Maribel, I'm Danny," I say, shaking her hand.

"Hi."

"Oh! And this is Bianca, she lives on our floor, too," Lea says, bouncing on her toes.

"Where are you going?" I ask.

"Maribel went to high school with a guy who lives in the baseball house, or a house where lots of baseball players live," Bianca answers.

"Oh! I bet that it's Gabe's brother's house!" I say, clapping my hands.

"Oh, you mean Lea's big dumb crush?" Bianca says. Lea gives her a look of death.

"You have a big dumb crush on Gabe?" I ask, raising an eyebrow.

She shrugs. "Maybe a little dumb crush."

"He is a fox," I say.

"He is. But you're right, he's probably gay," Lea says, shaking her head and looking sad.

"Aw, don't be sad, buttercup. He's a totally nice guy. Worthy of friendship, if nothing else," I say. My friends are all calling me back over. "I better go. But do you guys want to meet up tomorrow at the diner? I'll text you around noon?"

"Yeah, sure!" Lea enthuses.

"Cool, cool." I wave over my shoulder and head back across the street.

Casey *(Gabe's friend)*

I love my housemates, I really do, but it's nights like this one that kind of make me wish I had just gotten an apartment with Sam this year so that I wouldn't have to deal with a house full of friends of friends of friends on Halloween. It's fun, but there's something unsettling about it. Especially because there are so many masks this year. I don't ever remember seeing this many people in masks at a party before.

Gabe comes in around eleven. I told him he could bring whoever he wanted with him, but it kind of seems like he lost touch with his friends.

"What's with the bag?" I ask as he wanders in.

"I figure I'd crash here tonight," he says. "Sam said it was cool. . . ."

"Of course!"

He runs upstairs and I wait for him to come back before I get myself more beer.

"I thought you would have been here earlier," I say as he reappears.

"I decided to take a nap and that turned into like five hours of sleep," he says with a shrug.

"What on earth are you holding?"

"This?" he asks, holding up the oldest, creepiest, most moth-ridden werewolf mask I have ever seen.

"That's gross."

"I found it at my parents'," he says. "And you told me it was costumes required this year."

"So you're a decrepit werewolf?"

"Sure, let's go with that," he says, smirking. "Apparently all the chicks are really into those dudes on *Teen Wolf.*"

I blink at him. "Why do you know anything about *Teen Wolf*?"

"My little sisters told me that. Maybe they were lying."

"You look like Jason Bateman in *Teen Wolf Too.*"

"You're just jealous of my chest hair," he says. And to punctuate that statement he unbuttons the top button of his plaid shirt. "And at least I'm referencing current popular culture as opposed to eighties pop culture."

"Don't act like you've never seen those movies."

"Only because my dad owned them on VHS and we didn't have cable," Gabe says. "And who are you supposed to be?"

"I . . . am Batman," I say, pulling my cape around me with a flourish.

"You're wearing a cape with jeans."

"I am . . . casually neat Batman."

"Your Christian Bale voice needs work."

"I'm doing Michael Keaton," I say.

"And another outdated cultural reference! Not to mention that you don't sound like Michael Keaton. You think you do, but you don't."

I'll have to work on that, but I refuse to admit defeat. "So, want some beer?"

"Obviously."

"Do you need a chaperone, or can I hang here and greet people and you can come find me when you're done?"

"I'm good, I'll be right back."

Bailey, one of our other friends, comes in while Gabe is gone. "Who are you supposed to be?"

"I'm Dora the Explorer."

"Holy shit! You're Dora the Explorer!" I say as I fully take in the pink T-shirt and orange shorts.

"The T-shirt and shorts cost me seven dollars at Walmart and I stole this wig from my aunt."

"You probably should have shaved your legs."

"I thought about it, but I wasn't that invested."

"Good showing," I say, giving him a golf clap.

He shrugs and smiles. As a friend group I think we might shrug too much. "Where is Gabriel this evening?" he asks.

"Gone in search of beer," I say.

"How are his spirits?"

"They seem pretty good actually. I know we don't like . . . talk about him behind his back, and I'm sure he'll tell you about this, but I saw him last week at the dining hall and he said he started seeing a therapist."

"Whoa, wait," Sam's voice says behind me. "Who started seeing a therapist?"

"Your brother," I say, unable to hide the question in my voice.

"Oh, yeah. I knew that. It's a good idea, I think."

"I'm always the last one to find this stuff out," Bailey says.

Gabe comes up the stairs smiling and saying hi to people he passes. He gives Bailey one of the beers he was carrying.

"That's good service you have here," Bailey says to me.

"They were technically both for me," Gabe says. "But I suppose I'll share."

"What about me?" Sam says.

"You shouldn't drink anyway. Don't you have some kind of sport you're training for?" Gabe asks with a grin.

"Shut up, so do these two losers!" Sam retorts as he trudges downstairs.

The three of us back off out of the way and lean on the kitchen counter, bullshitting as we tend to do. Gabe and Bailey argue about Gabe's lack of costuming and Gabe pulls his mask on to demonstrate that it's not so bad at the same second Lea walks in.

I nudge him. "The girl of your dreams is here."

"Huh?"

"Lea. Is here."

"What? Where?" he asks, lifting his mask and leaning in to hear better.

"She just went into the basement."

"Shit. I hate the basement. It's so loud down there."

"It's a party, Grandma Gabe," Bailey says, tapping him on the chest. "We'll go find Sam."

"Come on, ten minutes of mingling never hurt anyone," I add.

Gabe makes a face but pulls back on his mask, and Bailey straightens his wig. We go down into the basement, where the lights are mostly off except for one in the far corner by the keg and a lit disco ball that my roommates hung up in the middle of the room. It seems to be spinning a little too fast, but that might be the four beers I've had.

"This doesn't even look like your basement," comes Gabe's muffled voice from behind his mask.

"I was just thinking the same thing!" I call back.

We wander around. Sam is talking to a girl I've never seen

before and he gestures for us to stay away. It's surprisingly packed down here.

Finally I see Lea and her two friends in the corner by the keg. Gabe sweeps in like nobody's business and starts pumping beer for them. I've never seen him this energetic about a girl before. The girls are talking and smiling, and I'm annoyed at him for being too stupid to take his mask off before jumping into the fray. Now Lea has no idea that her chivalrous beer pumper is actually Gabe. I shake my head.

"Dumbass should have taken his mask off," Bailey says loudly in my ear.

"Such a shame," I say.

I hear the girls thank him and then move away. Gabe saunters back over to us, head held high, back straight, obviously feeling like he just did something awesome. A minute later we all have fresh cups of beer and I gesture for us to head back upstairs. Gabe raises his mask as we enter the relatively quieter and much cooler kitchen, taking up our same positions by the counter from fifteen minutes ago.

"That was good, right?" Gabe says.

"Yeah, except she doesn't know it was you," Bailey says, smacking the back of his head.

"Oh, duh." He seems to consider this for a second. "I'll just wait here until she comes up to use the bathroom and hopefully she'll recognize my clothes?"

"I've heard worse plans," I say.

We take turns getting beer for the next couple of hours and eventually Gabe hops up on the counter, sitting and swinging his feet, talking to everyone who passes by as he gets a little drunk, and then a lot drunk. It's obvious that tons of people missed him last semester and I think this party is the first chance he's had to see that. He's chatting up one of the other housemates, so Bailey and I head down for more beer.

"I haven't seen him in this good of a mood in a long time," Bailey says.

"Yeah, I know. It's good, right?"

"Totally."

I see Lea head up the stairs with one of her friends and Bailey and I make a beeline. There's not much to see but at least she waves at Gabe and he waves back from his spot in the kitchen. I can tell she just made his night from the way he's smiling.

"You should go talk to her," I say.

He shakes his head. "I don't ever know what to say. It's dumb. And I'm so sloppy drunk now I would probably say something stupid."

"Sometimes it's better to say something stupid than nothing at all."

"That goes against my entire belief system," he says.

NOVEMBER

Sam *(Gabe's brother)*

"Where am I?" Gabe asks, sitting up on the floor, mildly breathless.

"You're in my bedroom," I tell him.

He looks over at me and rubs his eyes. "Holy shit, what happened last night?"

"You drank copiously, talked to everyone on Earth except for the girl you like, told multiple people that Jason Bateman was hands down the best Teen Wolf, and then you passed out on my bedroom floor around four in the morning."

He leans his elbows on his knees. "I don't remember much of that."

"I'm not surprised."

"I really didn't talk to Lea?"

"Nope."

"What's the point of becoming mind-numbingly drunk if it doesn't even give you the balls to talk to the girl you like?" he asks as I get up to grab water bottles out of the minifridge in my room.

"You waved bashfully at her several times."

He gives me a dirty look. "Where's Casey?"

"In the shower."

"Oh, man, I want to do that, too."

"He probably doesn't want to share his private time with you that way."

I get another dirty look. "What time is it?"

"Noon."

"How did I sleep for eight hours on the floor?"

"I don't know, but you were seriously loving up that bean-bag chair."

He stares at it like it just popped out of thin air. Then he looks back at me. "All right. So."

He squeezes his eyes shut.

"You okay?"

"Yup. A little spinny. And starving."

"You want to go to the diner?"

"Yes. As soon I shower and unseal my contacts from my eyes."

Casey comes in then.

"Dude," Casey says as they pass, tapping Gabe on the shoulder. "You were wasted last night, without a doubt the most drunk I have ever seen you."

Gabe shakes his head. "I was somewhere beyond wasted I think."

After all of us have showered the drunken night off us, we head out to the diner, where Lea and her friends are sitting three booths over. I would go so far as to call it serendipitous.

I raise my eyebrows at Gabe, and Casey lets out a low wolf whistle as we're seated.

"Please do not embarrass me," Gabe hisses.

"No promises," I say as I flip through the menu.

Maxine (a waitress)

Saturdays can be a real bitch. Depends on the time of year, but it can be packed in here from morning til night. And today's the day after Halloween, so we have all the usual hangovers and a football game. It's quite the mix of folks.

The girl and the boy from a few weeks ago are back and with just a little bit of eavesdropping I've learned their names, Gabe and Lea. Good names; I like the way they sound together.

Of course the manager is here, so I can't make up my own seating arrangements. Instead, one of the times I'm over by the boys refilling coffee, I tell them they should go over and chat the girls up if they're going to keep looking at them like that.

Gabe's eyes go wide in fear. "No, no. That's okay. No, thank you."

I let it rest; some men just have to do things in their own time. Gabe is apparently one of them. But if he takes too long, believe you me, I will take matters into my own hands some-day and send her a delicious, fresh-squeezed glass of orange juice, courtesy of that cutie pie.

Maribel (Lea's roommate)

"So, what are they doing now?" Lea whispers to me.

I'm the only one with a visual on Gabe's group, thanks to the fact that I'm the only one of us facing the mirrored wall in the back of the diner.

"They're working out the check. . . ." I say.

"So, Danny," Bianca says, narrowing her eyes. "Lea says you think Gabe is gay. But would a gay guy really dress like that?"

"Gay men come in a variety of shapes and fashion sense," he says with a grin. "What's the plural of fashion sense?"

"Fashions sense?" I offer.

"Fashion senses?" Bianca suggests.

"Senses of fashion," Lea says.

Bianca sighs. "And I know they come in a variety of senses of fashion. I guess I just want him and Lea to get together. But it's silly to root for them if there's no point."

"There really is no point," Lea says. "Even if he does like girls, he's totally into this girl Hillary in creative writing."

"Sounds like Hillary is a skank queen of Cockblock-ville," Danny says in a singsong voice.

"That's not nice," Lea says, trying not to laugh.

Bianca and I don't bother holding our giggles in.

"What are they doing now?" Lea asks.

"I think they're having trouble with the math," I say. "Maybe I should go offer to help them."

"Don't you dare!" Lea says.

I do love teasing her.

"His friends are cute," Bianca says, pointedly ignoring Lea.

"Guys," Lea pleads.

"Oh, Lea, calm down. I'm not going over there. But I was talking to the one guy last night, Sam? He's Gabe's brother. I bet he would be able to tell us whether or not Gabe is gay."

"You girls need to learn to trust me! I will not steer you wrong," Danny says.

Bianca tips her head in thought. "If you say so."

"Oh, I say so," he responds knowingly. I can already tell that I'm going to love Danny with all my heart, but I think he's wrong on this one. I just don't know him well enough to tell him how wrong I think he is.

I was watching the way Gabe was watching Lea during the party last night and I think he really likes her. I just don't know how to say that to Danny without hurting his feelings.

The group of boys walks out past us.

"I should have talked to him," Lea says, chin in hand, watching them go. "Or at least waved. As it stands now the last thing I said to him was 'thank you' the other day in class when he handed my paper back to me."

"At least you were polite," I say.

"Don't worry," Danny chimes in. "We'll still invite you to the wedding."

Inga (creative writing professor)

Cole and I meet once a week to go over what's been happening in office hours and to discuss general class-related business. I feel like I need to touch base with him and make sure there's nothing going on that he can't handle. But he's a pretty serious and responsible guy, so it hasn't been an issue.

I think he assumed these were going to be extremely thoughtful and erudite meetings regarding assignments and grading rubrics. And sometimes things of that nature come up. But more often than not it devolves into me telling him ridiculous stories about the weekend trips I take with Pam and him goading me on as I talk shit about all the students in the class.

He's aware of how much I like Gabe and Lea.

"You've gotten so in my head about that!" he tells me. "They came to see me one after another at office hours a week or two ago and I forgot that they're not actually dating. I told her not to keep her boyfriend waiting."

I sit up straight and at attention. "What happened?"

"Well, they both looked absolutely mortified and I awkwardly tried to cover up my mistake, and if it was embarrassing for me, I can't even imagine how they felt."

"Yikes."

He nods.

"I just can't believe that Hillary snagged him to work with," I say, shaking my head. My dislike for Hillary grows on a daily basis. I mean, half the reason I give these kinds of assignments is so my couple du jour will have a chance to interact. How much more can I do? I'm going to have to trick them into going on a date with each other. Tell them it's mandatory office hours and then reveal a well-appointed table with the world's most romantic foods and then sneak out the door.

"Yeah, that was quite the coup."

I shake my head. "I wish I could make them realize they're meant for each other. Time's a-wasting! The semester will not last forever!"

"We could try to convince them to take creative writing part two," Cole suggests.

I look at him appraisingly. "I knew there was a reason I

liked you. I knew there was a reason you were my TA."

He smiles.

"You're like a genius at this, Cole. Who knew you had such a knack for classroom romance?"

"I definitely had no clue," he says. "You think I could put that on my résumé?"

"I'll be sure to mention it in every reference letter I write for you."

"Thanks," he says.

"Now, we have one more issue at hand."

He looks at me like I'm about to say something very serious.

"How do we keep Hillary out of the second part of creative writing?"

Bob (a bus driver)

Look at these two. On alone, off alone, walking alone. I wish they could be together. No one so young should be so alone all the time.

And I suppose they have friends in other places, and that I'm only seeing a tiny sliver of their lives, but it seems to me if they're moving in the same direction, why not move in the same direction together? I'm not talking about undying love, but I wish they would at least become friends. That wouldn't be too hard.

I have to admit that they kind of, sort of remind me of me and my wife, Margie, back in the day. I can't put my finger on why exactly, but I was also a tall gangly kid, so maybe that's a start.

Makes me wish I was a matchmaker, or knew some way to make them talk to each other. Maybe one day the bus will be really crowded and they'll be standing next to each other and I'll stop short and she could fall into his arms.

I'm obviously getting sappy in my old age. Maybe I'll take the wife away to the Poconos for Thanksgiving weekend or something.

Squirrel!

The girl has come back to me!

Hooray!

I race over to her where she's sitting on the bench. I preen for her, fluffing my tail. I hope she recognizes me. I hope she has more peanuts.

"Hey there, little guy," she says.

I scamper closer.

"Are you the same squirrel I always talk to?"

I don't know what you're saying but I'm sure I love you!

We are going to be best friends. Maybe she has a house she will take me to and she will let me roam around and sleep in her bed. I've heard about beds and I think they sound magnificent.

"Do you like bagels?" she asks.

I stand up straight and look her in the eye. I have no idea what a bagel is. But it sounds like a type of nut to me.

She tosses me a crumb.

It's not a nut. It's like bread.

This is disappointing but only for a minute because it's also delicious.

She tosses me another crumb.

"I'm waiting for my friend," she says. "Do you have friends? Or a family? What's life like for a little squirrel such as yourself?"

She tosses me one more crumb and brushes off her hands.

"There he is! See you next time," she says to me.

What a wonderful person.

Danny (Lea's friend)

"Hello, Azalea Fong!"

"Hey, Danny!" she says, popping off the bench. "You're the only person I would let get away with calling me Azalea. Besides my mom. But she so rarely gets in touch lately that it's probably not worth mentioning."

I make a frowny face.

"Enough about suckiness. What's up with you?" she asks.

"First of all, were you just talking to that squirrel?"

She turns to look over her shoulder. "He's my friend."

"Okey dokey," I say with a nod.

"I like squirrels," she says with a shrug.

"Moving on, I would like to complain about the weather."

"Proceed," she says, her face serious.

"It is freaking cold outside today! Wasn't it summer like last Tuesday?"

"I know you're saying that as hyperbole, but seriously, last Tuesday it was seventy-five degrees outside and today it's barely forty. So, it's true, last Tuesday was essentially summer compared to this."

"Thank you, my favorite literal person."

"What's on the agenda today?"

"Well, considering how much luck I always have seeing Gabe when I'm with you, I thought perhaps today would be a perfect time for another round of stalking him."

"Delightful," she says, pausing at the fork in the path. "Though you realize I can't actually make him appear."

"Yes. I need to check my school PO box. How about we start there?"

"Sounds like a plan, man," she says. She's quiet for a few minutes while we walk.

"Whatcha thinking about?" I ask.

She sighs. "I'm just jealous that Gabe is working with this girl in creative writing. And I want to work with him."

"I understand. How does he act around her?"

"Like Gabe," she says with a shrug. "Quiet and nice and he smiles a lot at her."

"That does sound quite Gabe-ish," I say, as we walk into the post office. "Holy crap. It's like invoking his name makes him appear!"

She smiles and watches as Gabe gets a couple of envelopes out of his mailbox. He must feel us looking at him because he glances over and waves.

"I suppose I could try being friends with him, at least talking to him in class and stuff. He's cute and quiet and I like how . . . he behaves, all polite."

"He's so cute," I mumble.

"Totally," she agrees. "Would it be wrong to use the word 'dreamy'?"

"Definitely not."

He heads off in a different direction, and Lea and I turn back toward the bus stop.

"We could have stalked him longer," she says.

"No, it's cool, sometimes I just need a taste."

I know she gets it, even if she does look really sad.

I can admit, there's a small chance that I'm deluding myself about his sexual preference. But really, there aren't that many straight guys who compliment other guys' jeans.

Inga (creative writing professor)

Part of me always feels bad when I make the kids read their stories or essays aloud in class. But another part of me knows that it's a great habit to get into. Reading your work aloud makes you see all different nuances. There's a big difference in the way we write compared to the way we speak, and the only way to learn that is to hear it. The best way to do that is to read everything you write out loud.

I recommend they start by reading aloud to something inanimate, and then move on to their friend or their mom. And then it's time to read in front of the class. Nearly every class period someone has shared their work, if not multiple someones. Everyone except Gabe.

He talked to both Cole and me about how nervous he is to share anything with the class. He and I worked to get his childhood memory essay just right, and to the point where sharing it with other people doesn't make him want to hide under his desk.

He came to see me after Hillary critiqued it and said that he wanted to drop the class. She had told him that he wasn't an interesting writer. I said that I feel like he's a talented writer, with a different style that not everyone can appreciate. I was proud of myself because what I wanted to say was something more along the lines of disparaging Hillary and everything she stands for.

I walk over to his desk and smile at him before class starts.

"Listen, if you don't want to read it, I'll read it for you," I offer, even though I shouldn't. It's already the week before Thanksgiving and he's gone almost the entire semester without reading anything to the class.

"No, no," he says, picking at the edge of the desk. "I'll do it. I need to man up."

"It's a great story. Your use of metaphor is spot-on."

"If I throw up, just try not to make a big deal of it, okay?"

"How have you made it this far in life without having to give so many presentations that you aren't at least a little bit desensitized?"

"Honestly? I've had to give a lot, but it's like it gets worse every time instead of better."

I make a sympathetic face and then call the class to order.

"Gabe's going to share his assignment from a couple of weeks ago, about a childhood memory, so give him your attention."

I grab a seat in the first row and I hear Victor mutter behind me, "About damn time."

Gabe stands in front of the class, trying so hard to make himself small, which somehow manages to make him seem even taller and more gangly. He cracks his knuckles and then smiles at the class. I can see the paper waver in his hands. But he pushes through his nerves and he starts to read.

There's a picture on the Internet of a tree that's grown around a bicycle. The story goes that a boy left his bike leaning against the tree and then forgot all about it when he was called off to war. That's not really the true story, but if you've never seen this picture, you should go home and Google it. It's fascinating.

It always makes me think of this one time that my mom and I were at the food store when I was about six years old. It was memorable in part because it was so rare that my mom took me anywhere all by myself. My older brother was almost always there, or one of my younger sisters. But I don't know if I was home from school sick, or if maybe my dad was watching the other kids, but this day sticks out because it was her and me.

An old man started talking to my mom and then he turned to me and asked me my name. I hid behind my mom because I was really scared of strangers. I think we may have watched too many stranger-danger videos in kindergarten, so that on top of my innate shyness made talking to people I didn't know almost impossible.

This old man was one of those scary old men, at least to six-year-old me. He looked like his skin was melting off his face and he smelled weird. What was left of his hair was long and scraggly, and his shirt was misbuttoned.

In the car on the way home, my mom asked me why I was so scared, and said that I didn't have to be. She knew the old man and he was her neighbor when she was little like me. I explained about his skin and his hair and his disheveled nature as well as I could with my limited six-year-old vocabulary.

She said, "Oh, that's okay, Gabe. You'll grow out of that. You won't always feel so scared and shy around grown-ups."

I remember thinking that day that I'll always be scared, that I don't understand how not to be scared. As I got older I thought about that day all the time. It was only very recently that I realized my mom was right, but not in the way she thought.

I did lose some of my wariness and my fear as I matured, but I've never quite shaken my shyness. When I think about it, it's like I would have never been able to grow out of it. It's like the tree and the bicycle. I grew around it and it became part of me.

When he's done he glances at the classroom through his eyelashes and slinks back to his seat. I keep myself from giving him a standing ovation. When I glance over at Lea, she's literally grinning into her hands and I can see hearts coming out of her eyes. She is the picture of a girl falling in love. There's no way they're not getting together now.

Sam (Gabe's brother)

I'm standing outside the English building waiting for Gabe to emerge so we can finally go home for Thanksgiving. I pleaded with him to skip this class so we could leave before rush hour but he insisted he needed to see Lea.

She comes out ahead of him and I smile at her.

"Hey," she says, her voice more a question than a greeting.

"Hi," I respond with a smile.

Gabe comes out the door right behind her and he looks stricken at our passing words.

"Yo," I say to him, as I glance over my shoulder at Lea walking away.

"Were you talking to her?"

"She said hey, I said hi. We're not exactly best friends."

He exhales the obvious breath he'd been holding and we head in the direction of the parking lot.

"Do you need to stop by your building?"

"Yeah. Sorry. I didn't really want to drag all my crap with me to class."

"Understandable. But the longer we sit in traffic, the longer you're going to have to listen to my musical choices. And you're not going to complain."

He rolls his eyes as we get in the car.

"We should have offered to give Lea a ride to your building."

"I can't even imagine how painful that car ride would be.

With me saying nothing and her . . ." He squeezes his eyes shut like the world is far too terrible.

"What? What's wrong?" I ask as I start the car.

He shakes his head. "I read this assignment out loud in class today, about how shy I am. She probably thinks I'm a complete loser now."

"Nah, girls dig that crap."

"Seriously? You think so?"

"Yeah, they love all that sensitive, sentimental stuff."

"I don't think there's a single woman on Earth who would appreciate you lumping them together that way. Except maybe Hillary. That girl is a ridiculous caricature of everything that's wrong with the world."

"I'm impressed, Gabe."

"With what?"

"I had no idea you were a feminist, or that you used words like 'caricature.' "

He punches my arm.

"Hey, hands off the driver," I joke, laughing.

His face goes ashen.

"Gabe. It's a joke. No big deal."

"I know, I know." He chews his thumbnail and looks out the window, watching the buildings pass while I curse myself for making a driving joke. "Just . . . be careful."

DECEMBER

Charlotte (a barista)

The place is packed, as it usually is at this point in the afternoon, but the line is suspiciously short so I let one of the other people take their break before me, hoping that when it's my turn to take a break it'll be in the middle of chaos and I'll get to walk away casually, like Mel Gibson as a bomb goes off behind him.

Maybe I should pick someone cooler than Mel Gibson.

I'll work on that.

It's another terrible shift without Keith or Tabitha. Tabitha would be particularly effusive and happy today since Lea is here, which means any second Gabe is going to wander in.

And like clockwork, there he is. He glances over at her and then steps into the line.

I'm feeling a little more neutral about him recently. I'm not sure way. Perhaps I've been infused with the Christmas spirit or I've finally just lost my mind. I'm on drink duty, so I probably won't have a chance to talk to him. He's a regular coffee kind of guy. I'm almost a little disappointed because I'd like to test him, see if he's more normal these days.

Shockingly, he orders a mint hot chocolate. I'm so surprised that I'm actually going to get to make his drink that I almost drop the cup when I see the "Gabe" scrawled on the side. He walks down to the end of the counter and leans casually out of the way.

"Hey," I say to him.

He nods at me, smiling a little, tight-lipped.

"Mint hot chocolate?" I say.

He stares at my lips. I don't think I've ever had anyone stare at my lips quite so intently. Not even the kid who stalked me sophomore year of high school.

"It's good stuff here; I'll add a little extra pump of mint for you and make it even better," I tell him conspiratorially. He continues to stare at my lips but he draws his eyebrows down even farther in confusion. He probably can't hear me over the steam wand at the moment.

"How's the end of the semester going?" I try a new tact with him.

He shrugs.

"Yeah, I feel that." This isn't going nearly as well as I had expected and I can feel burgeoning hope for him and Lea ebb and fade. Damn Tabitha, she brainwashed me.

"Whip?" I ask.

He draws his eyebrows in even more, squinting, and then it's like he gives up.

"I'm sorry?" he says finally, looking me in the eye.

"Do you want whipped cream?" I ask, holding up the bottle.

"Oh, yeah." He pauses, licking his lips. "I have trouble hearing in here sometimes."

"That's cool. It's loud."

He smiles and nods as he accepts his drink. "Thanks," he says.

The line is even quieter now and I have no drinks stacked waiting for me, so I watch Gabe pick his way across the room. There aren't too many empty tables. There's a two-seater right next to Lea and I think maybe he's going to take that one. He stops and stares at it even, and I feel like his thoughts are written all over his face, calculating some kind of impossible math problem that involves how to get himself into that seat. He changes course and ends up farther away from her, but as he sits she looks up.

They wave at each other.

She glances at the seat he didn't take and I wonder what

the deal is with them. Not in the silly way that we gossip about, but I wonder about the way that they look at each other but so rarely acknowledge it. It's kind of sad. I promise myself I'll go back to being annoyed by them tomorrow, but for now I let myself sink into the melancholy.

But then there are two salted caramel lattes to make, and a venti white chocolate mocha, and a break that's coming up any second and the bell jingling on the door. Their moment is over and so is mine.

Frank (Chinese food delivery guy)

Back to the freshman dorm with another delivery. Seriously, these two need to get their acts together and order at the same time. I'm getting tired of driving out here twice in the same day. It's the third time in two months.

"Hey," I say as the girl comes to collect her order.

"Hey," she responds, handing me her money.

"So, you and your boyfriend have a fight?"

"Who?" she asks, side-eyeing me.

"You know, the kid who lives upstairs."

"Gabe? He's not my boyfriend." She says it fast and I feel like I've been around long enough to know that her quick denial means she probably likes him.

"He ordered like an hour ago, same stuff as last time. You should start ordering together."

"But we're not together," she insists.

"That's not really what I'm saying."

"I'm confused."

"I'm not exactly Dear Abby, but you guys have . . . something weird going on. I can tell. I have a third eye."

She gives me a vaguely disgusted look.

"You know, like I can see shit. And there's something about you guys. I don't know. Call me crazy, but I think if you asked him to order food with you, he'd be into it."

"I . . ." She pauses and shakes her head. "Thanks."

She walks away then and I feel like a royal dumbass. But I had to say something. My grandma would be so mad at me if I didn't. She's the one who taught me about the third eye.

Hillary (creative writing classmate)

It's the last day of creative writing for the semester. I can't believe it's over and Gabe still hasn't asked me out. I mean, what is that about? I thought for sure he was super into me.

Inga calls the class to attention and hands back a big stack of papers that she'd apparently been hoarding. And then she makes the last two people in the class read for the semester. When they're done she claps her hands together.

"All right guys, this is it. I want to remind you that your final papers are due one week from today. And I want hard copies of them, not just emailed at some random moment when you blur the deadline. I'll be in my office from ten to twelve next Tuesday, or you can drop it in my mailbox in the English department anytime between now and then."

Victor groans. I have to admit that I have a lot of respect for Victor. He always speaks his mind.

"A problem, Victor?"

"Such a waste of trees," he says.

Inga glares at him. "For final papers I like to have hard copies."

"I don't mean—" He stops, rolls his eyes. "Whatever."

Inga stares at him for another second and I hope he keeps going. I love the drama.

"Anyway, these are long papers. In the past when I accepted emailed documents I often found myself printing them out anyway. I might seem like a dinosaur to you, but there's something about seeing your work on the page as opposed to the screen. I think I mark better on paper. People get higher grades."

Victor plasters a huge fake smile on his face.

"Anything else?" Inga asks.

Silence.

I notice Gabe is antsy, his feet kicking the back of Victor's chair. I can almost see the steam rising from Victor's ears. Inga definitely doesn't notice.

"Well, then class dismissed. I know it's a little early, so I'll take questions here and now if you have any; if not I'd suggest taking this found time to work on your final."

Victor wheels around in his seat as soon as Inga's done and first stares at Lea and then stares at Gabe.

"Listen, if you two like each other so damn much, you should probably just get it on already and stop annoying all the people around you."

I gasp. I can't help it. I almost laugh, because seriously, how could Victor think that Gabe and Lea have any chemistry. They look at each other for a second and then Gabe pretty much runs out of the classroom. Lea takes her time packing up, and Victor continues to mutter under his breath.

I guess Gabe isn't going to ask me out.

Victor (creative writing classmate)

Midnight breakfast is definitely one of my favorite nights of the year. I don't know why it all tastes so much better at midnight than it does in the morning, but seriously, it's just genius. I'm going to spend the whole damn night eating toast and omelets and hash browns.

I'm so excited I don't even notice one of my least-favorite people ahead of me in line. But there's the Giraffe, ordering more than her fair share of triangle hash browns.

And as she's walking toward the drink station, Big Foot himself comes through, colliding with her.

Of course.

Her full food tray and his mostly empty one fall to the ground with a crash, scattering glass and food everywhere.

I weep for all those hash browns.

I step off to the side.

Their mess is blocking my way and, really, I don't want to deal with them right now. Hopefully a custodian will come soon and they'll be on their way. Because I definitely don't feel bad about what I said to them earlier, but it's not like I want to challenge Big Foot to a fight over his woman's honor or something. He's totally that kind of guy.

I back away, concealed in a gap between the wall and the soda dispenser, and I listen to the two of them chirp apologies at each other.

"I'm so sorry," she says.

"No, no, it was me," he says.

Why am I stuck here listening to this? It's gotta be karmic retribution, but I don't even know for what. I'm a good guy! I get a little impatient sometimes, but who doesn't?

"You're kneeling in syrup," she says, her voice all weird and breathy like it's some kind of beautiful phrase that should be cross-stitched on a pillow or something.

Apparently he doesn't respond because I hear her again. "Your knee."

"Oh, nobigdeal," he says quietly.

Can these two just stop? I try to find an escape route, but there's just no way through. I could try to cut around them, but they're blocking the entire archway. And I guess everyone else is avoiding this area due to the mess, so there's no one to even use as a diversion.

"I just wanted to make sure you weren't kneeling in any glass," she says, still using her cross-stitch voice.

"I'm not." Maybe I like him more than I thought I did. He keeps things succinct, to the point. I peek around the corner and he's making these sad eyes at her and I take back my previous thought. And I wonder if I'm ever going to get out of here. I peek again.

"I think there are some little shards over here," he says.

"Yeah, but I think you got everything in this spot."

"Are you okay?"

"Yeah, fine. You?"

"Yeah, except for my jeans . . ." he says with this dumb-shit little smile.

The custodian finally comes over here and I think these two might get out of the way. But instead they stand there and decide to have a little chat. Perfect.

First they have to apologize profusely to the janitor, who waves them off and says they did a good job. People need to stop being so nice to them.

Then in the biggest moment of idiocy I have ever encountered, the Giraffe turns to Big Foot and says, all fluttering eyelashes and adoring gazes, "I'm Lea. I feel like we should have properly introduced ourselves like a hundred years ago."

I want to slam my head into the wall. Why won't they go away?

"Gabe."

I shake my head and roll my eyes and just barely keep from concussing myself into oblivion.

"I kept meaning to talk to you in class, but it seemed weird, like we already knew each other, or already should have known each other. And the longer I waited the weirder it felt and then we lived in the same building and you didn't really seem like you wanted to talk, and I didn't want to bother you. I'm going to stop talking now."

I stare at the ceiling, praying for it to fall on me.

"I, um . . . didn't want to bother you either."

"Well, now that we've both said it that way, maybe we should start bothering each other."

I pick up my fork off my tray and pretend to stab myself in the eye with it.

"I'm gonna go."

THANK GOD.

"Sure, sure," she says.

"Are you leaving? We could, um, walk together."

JUST GO.

"Ah, no. Maribel, my roommate, she's over there and we're

going to stay here and study for a little longer. I was getting us extra hash browns to share."

"Okay."

"I'll see you around though?"

"Yeah, sure."

I am almost going to get out of here. I feel like I'm about to be released from prison. I might actually kiss the ground after this.

"Gabe?"

No.

"Yeah?"

"I really liked your essay. About being shy? I mean, I liked all the work of yours I've read, but that one was really good."

He doesn't say anything.

"I looked up that tree on the Internet. It's fascinating."

He makes a weird, choked laughing sound. Maybe I should put him out of his misery, too.

"Anyway, if I don't see you, have a good break," she says.

"Yeah, you too."

Finally. I make my way back to my friends, who don't even seem to notice I've been gone that long. And of course my omelet is cold.

———————————

Maribel (Lea's roommate)

"Hey, where have you been?" I ask as Lea comes back to our table. "I thought you abandoned me and I was going to have to slink out of here with all of our crap by myself. You have a lot of crap." I survey the table. She's got stacks of notebooks and index cards and highlighters. I think she has a serious school-supply addiction.

She shakes her head, a smile threatening to burst off her face. "The most amazing thing just happened."

"Really? What? Are they making smoothies?" I ask, leaning around her, trying to see the food area. "I heard there are supposed to be smoothies. And weren't you getting us more hash browns?"

"Maribel," Lea says seriously. "Gabe was here."

"Oh! Fun!" I say. It's only sort of fun. This is going to be another one of those stories about how she gazed at him adoringly while he stared out the window or something. That's how a lot of the Gabe stories go these days. I've been thinking that I might have to counsel her into finding a new object of affection.

"We talked," she says, her eyes wide.

That is not what I expected. "What happened? Leave no detail behind."

"All right," she says, composing herself and folding her hands on the table, leaning close to divulge. "So, I finished going back through the line to get more of the triangle hash browns, and I was thinking about how delicious they were, so I didn't look both ways to see if I was walking in front of anyone."

"That is so unlike you. You're such a stickler for pedestrian traffic rituals, even indoors."

"I know, right?" she says. "So, out from the other side comes Gabe and we collide, sending our trays to the floor and making a huge gross mess."

"Oh no!" I say, though inwardly I'm relieved that I didn't have to deal with the mess. I'm kind of a terrible friend sometimes.

"He immediately drops down and starts cleaning it up, picking up pieces of plates and cups. I grab the garbage can and bring it closer and then get some napkins to try to clean up all the drinks. When I crouch next to him he says he's sorry. And then we both just kind of keep saying sorry over and over again. And I tell him he's kneeling in maple syrup and he doesn't hear me at first and then he says it's no big deal."

I nod along with the story because I have a sense that it's going somewhere.

"Then the janitor comes up and says he'll take it from there. And Gabe puts his hand out to help me up!"

"That's really cute," I say, and I mean it. I smile then and assume that's got to be the end of this story.

"And then!" she says, her eyes going wide.

"Whoa, whoa, whoa, there's an 'and then'?"

"Yes! More than one even!" she exclaims. "Gabe kind of lingers, wiping his hands, so I linger and I decide to introduce myself since I haven't ever, really. And he says he's Gabe. And then I babble about how I wanted to talk to him in the past but I didn't want to bother him or anything. And then basically when I feel like I'm probably going to die from embarrassment he says he didn't want to bother me either."

She pauses, beaming, and again I think that must be the end of the story. It's a good story considering they've never spoken to each other before.

"And then he basically asked me if I wanted to walk home with him!"

"Why did you say no?"

"Because you're here and I didn't want to abandon you."

"Damn me! And being here! And you being a good friend and not abandoning me."

"It's okay, Mar. It probably would have been really awkward."

"Or maybe not," I say.

"And then I told him I liked his essay and that I looked up that tree online and he looked so embarrassed. In conclusion, I want to hug him."

"I like that conclusion," I say, grinning.

"He's so shy. Like I knew he was shy, but somehow, up close like that, where it was just us, he seemed even more than shy. Tense and afraid. I think he was almost relieved when I said that I had to stay."

"That makes sense from what you told me about him."

"And then I would have gone into my awkward-and-reserved mode, or even worse, trying-to-fill-the-void-of-silence mode, and it would have been a terrible walk."

I look at her sympathetically. Those are two modes that she falls into quite often.

"Oh, God, I like him so much. What am I going to do?" she says, flailing dramatically and slumping in her chair.

"Is it finally time to take action?" I ask, slamming my fist on the table.

She sits up straight. "I think it is. But Danny said he's not into girls. There's no changing that."

"We need confirmation on that. It's the one piece of the puzzle that's not quite coming together. We'll figure this out, okay?"

"You're so nice to me. Why are you so nice to me?"

"Because," I say, shrugging. "We'll get Bianca on it too. She's great with this stuff. She's like a CSI agent, putting together pieces of mysterious boys' lives for the greater good."

"It's so stupid to like him this much. I was doing fine until he read that essay in class."

"Lea, calm down. We're going to do this and you're going to be so happy."

"You know, normally, I would be like, that's great, but what if he's a jerk? But I know he's not a jerk."

"No, he's quite obviously not a jerk."

"Ugh, you know who totally is a jerk though?"

"Who?"

She tips her chin a few tables over.

"Who is that?"

"Victor from creative writing."

"The one who was a douche to you guys the other day?"

"Yup."

"Damn him."

"Damn him indeed."

Casey (Gabe's friend)

Gabe's twenty-first birthday is in the midst of finals. I feel kind of bad, because there's just no way I can go out hard for him in the middle of my exams, but we find a random afternoon that we both have free to at least go to the bar together for cheap slices and drafts.

"Happy birthday," I say, holding up my mug to clink with his.

"Thanks," he says before taking a sip. "Sucks that Sam couldn't come."

"It does, but he promises he'll make it up to you."

"I think I'm scared."

I laugh. "When are you finished with finals?"

"I had an in-class exam for two of my classes, I had one

final this morning, then I have a stats final on Monday, and I still have to hand in my creative writing paper on Thursday."

"Have you finished the paper?"

"Haven't even started it," he says around a bite of pizza. "I wanted to work on everything else first. The other classes I was worried about. I think I have this one in the bag. I'm still about to have an anxiety attack about stats."

"Want me to help you with it this weekend?"

"Yeah, that would be great," he says. "My head gets all jumbled."

I nod.

"I, um. I talked to Lea last night," he says.

"And you waited all this time to tell me!"

"We've been hanging out for like ten minutes."

"Still, ten minutes too long."

"She was . . . really nice."

"As usual."

"We were at midnight breakfast," he says.

"Why wasn't I invited to midnight breakfast?"

"I didn't think you'd want to go."

"You should have texted me."

"Fine, I'll keep that in mind for the next time."

"Good. I'm glad you're learning."

"We literally bumped into each other. It was mostly my fault. My elbow just completely gave out."

I nod sympathetically. "That damn elbow."

"It pretty much ruined my life," he says, rolling his eyes. "But now at least it gave me a chance to talk to Lea."

"Glass half full."

"Anyway. After we finished cleaning up, she was so . . . cute. She introduced herself like we didn't know each other. But it was so unassuming."

I smile. "Sounds like your kind of chick."

"Seriously. And she said something about not wanting to bother me, and I had to keep myself from like yelling at her that she could never bother me. But instead I said something about how I didn't want to bother her either. And then we kind of both stood there for a minute." He shakes his head, blushing. "I offered to walk her home, but her friend was there so they were staying."

He stares at the table.

"Sounds like a good interaction."

"It was. She said she liked the essay I read in class."

"A very good interaction."

"Do you think it was too much? Me asking to walk her home?"

"Not at all. You live in the same place. It was thoughtful. I'd go so far as to call it gentlemanly."

"Cool." He pauses, scratching his head. "I had a lot of trouble hearing her."

I nod, but stay quiet, because between this and the elbow thing I think he might talk about something substantial.

He's like a deer; I don't want to make any sudden movements and startle his thoughts away.

"It's like, I get so nervous. And I don't know where to look. And my ear is saying, 'Watch her mouth,' and my eyes are like, 'Look anywhere but at her mouth!' It's hard to break the habit of years and years of not looking at people."

Oh, man, he looks so sad. I don't know how to help him with this. He doesn't usually talk like this, and now I'm panicking and I have no idea what to say. I am the worst friend ever.

Maybe I'll make a joke?

"What about your nose? Does your nose get a say in the matter? Or your toenails, Gabe?"

"Shut up, don't be an asshole," he says, but he's smiling now at least. And at least he's not offended by my teasing.

"I think your left nut has an opinion, too."

He laughs. "I know it's dumb."

"It's not dumb," I say, shrugging. "It's a little arbitrary. You have to do what's good for you in the moment. And don't obsess about it."

"Yeah, you're right."

"I'm always right."

"She's like . . . really pretty, even prettier up close."

"I have to point out that you've seen her up close a bunch of times."

"Yeah, but this was different," he says, smiling. Then he

screws up his face in pain and pinches the bridge of his nose. "My essay was kind of lame. About being shy. I feel stupid now because she remembers it. And associates me with the lameness."

"I think that could probably work in your favor."

"Sam kind of said the same thing." He looks up at me, his face relaxing. "How do you figure?"

"'Cause it means she already knows you're shy and it's obvious she didn't think it was lame if she brought it up."

"Huh, I hadn't thought of it like that," he says, looking impressed. "Want another slice?"

"Definitely."

When he comes back to the table, I can't keep my mouth shut. "You know I only tease you like that 'cause you're awesome, right?"

"Yeah, whatever."

"No, I'm serious, Gabe. I'm sorry if you thought I was like minimizing anything. I just want you to not get so down on yourself," I say, measuring my words carefully.

"I know. I'm working on it."

"Cool."

He nods and takes a deep breath. "Can you maybe help me with this Lea thing? I don't know what I'm doing."

"Of course," I say. "I'll tutor you in stats and getting the ladies."

"You're such a dork," he says. "Forget I asked. I'm going to get Bailey's help."

"No way!"

"Or Sam."

"I score way more chicks than Bailey and Sam put together!"

He makes a dubious face and we move on to other topics.

Squirrel!

It smells like snow and I can't remember where I hid all of my acorns.

The boy and girl are walking toward each other but don't see each other yet and I hope they smile.

I think they're going to smile.

I wonder if they know where all of my acorns went.

They get to the walkway of a building and they look at each other for a minute, just standing there in the cold.

"Hi, Gabe."

"Hi, Lea."

Then I remember that I hid them behind a gigantic bush last time I saw this boy and this girl. But last time I saw this boy and this girl they didn't say anything to each other. Maybe now they're going to be friends!

Acorns are my friends!

———————

Inga (creative writing professor)

Something makes me look up from the paper I'm grading and through my office window I see Gabe and Lea standing outside red faced and smiling. I can't believe they're here at the same time. I feel giddy to the point that I should be embarrassed. No one should feel this invested in a couple they aren't a part of.

I tell myself to be cool as I wait the endless moments for them to walk down the hallway to my office. Then I see him pull the door open for her.

"Hey, guys!" I say as they walk in.

"Hi," Lea says.

Gabe waves.

"We, um. I mean, I am turning in my paper. I don't know why Gabe is here," Lea says, her face getting redder.

"I'm here to do that, too," he jumps in.

"You guys didn't come together?" I ask, my heart sinking a tiny bit.

"No, no, we ran into each other outside," Lea explains. But she still can't keep her eyes off Gabe as he goes through the folder in his backpack.

"Is it snowing out yet?" I ask, wanting to keep them here a little longer.

"No," Lea says, shaking her head. "It smells like it could."

"Like it could what?" Gabe asks, looking at Lea.

"Like it might snow," she tells him.

"I didn't know it was supposed to snow."

"They said it might flurry," she explains.

"It's cold enough," Gabe says.

I feel like I'm intruding on their conversation, mundane as it is, but they're still both holding on to their final papers for dear life and I don't want to interrupt them. For all I know I might have the chance to see them set up their first date right this very second. I look back and forth between them like it's Wimbledon.

"Um, are you done with finals?" Lea asks. Be still my heart, I think she might actually be asking him to hang out right in front of me. I have never been lucky enough to be privy to this moment before. Calm down, Inga, be still, don't scare them away.

He pulls off his beanie, revealing some impressive hat hair. "I, um, yes."

"Are you going to be around tonight? I think my friends and I are going out."

His shoulders droop and he frowns. "It was my birthday last week," he says. "I promised my mom I would be home for dinner tonight. Because I didn't see them then. She baked a cake and everything. I, uh, well . . ." He pauses, and I hope Lea can see how regretful he is. That he's not making up an excuse.

"Happy birthday last week," she says, smiling.

"Thanks," he says, also smiling. Then he shakes out of his

stupor. "We should hand in our papers."

"Oh, yeah, duh," Lea says, but she keeps her eyes on him an extra moment.

"No big deal. You guys are the first ones to make it in this morning," I tell them.

They both smile, but keep shooting sidelong glances at each other as they hand me their finals.

"I hope you're both going to take part two next semester. I think you're great writers. I think you would benefit from the second part of this course. It's designed with more of a workshop feel than the first part. More peer critiquing and discussion."

Now it's Gabe's turn to blush. "Thank you," he says, not looking at me.

"Thanks; I signed up," Lea says.

"You did?" Gabe asks, turning toward her.

"Yeah."

"I might, too," he tells me.

"Good, then I'll look forward to seeing you both in January."

They leave after that, but they pause just outside the door so I get to hear a little more of their conversation.

"I am really sorry I can't go out tonight," he says, his voice so sheepish I can totally picture the face he's making.

"That's cool."

He clears his throat. "Maybe, um, maybe some other time."

She smiles. "Sure, I mean, the semester's over, but there's always next semester."

"Yeah, or maybe I'll see you next time Casey has a party or something. That would be . . . cool." His voice is hard to make out because he's speaking so quietly. I curse my windowless door. Although I realize I shouldn't because I'm awfully lucky to have a window looking out to the green.

Their voices trail away down the hall.

I have a feeling there's still a solid chance of them getting together. It's just taking a little longer than I expected. But it'll happen.

Maribel (Lea's roommate)

"I want to get drunk tonight," Bianca says resolutely as we're walking to the bar.

"I'm pretty sure you're well on your way there," I say.

"Are you guys sure this is a good idea?" Lea asks for the millionth time.

"Yeah, of course. I asked around. This is the bar that never turns away fake IDs. Some of the bigger ones down the street follow the rules a lot closer, but as long as you have a decent fake, these guys just want to sell some liquor."

"I feel like I might puke," she says as we approach the door.

"You look like it, too," I say.

She twists her gloved hands together nervously.

"Come on. How many times do I have to say this? I've already been here once, testing it out, and there were zero problems. Just don't act so nervous."

We walk in and the place is nearly full. It'll be easy to get lost in the sea of faces as soon as we get past the bouncer. He barely even glances at our IDs before he waves us through. Lea smiles like someone has a gun to her back, but the guy must not be great at reading facial expressions.

We find a booth in the back, far from the bar, but quite frankly, who cares. At least we're in.

I buy the first celebratory round and immediately notice that Gabe's friend Casey is at the bar by himself, chatting with the bartender. I tip my chin toward him in a cool, hands-free greeting, and then head back to the girls with our drinks.

"Casey's here," I mutter.

"Casey as in Gabe's Casey?" Lea asks, taking a sip through her straw.

"Yes."

"Ah-may-zing!" Bianca says, slamming her fist on the table. "Maybe Gabe is here, too." She starts twisting around, trying to catch sight of every last person in the bar.

"How much did you pregame?" I ask Bianca.

She gives me a look of pure crazy-eyes, which I translate to mean "a lot."

When she offers to go up and get the next round, I keep a close eye on her. As soon as I realize that she's talking to

Casey, Lea and I are hot on her heels. Because who knows what she might end up saying.

"I know who you are," she's cooing as we approach.

"Oh yeah? Who am I?"

"You're Gabe's friend."

His eyes light up. "That is correct. I'm Casey."

"I'm Bianca, it's my birthday," she tells him as they shake hands.

"Happy birthday!"

"It's not her birthday," Lea says, rolling her eyes at Casey. He grins widely but seems to want to continue to play along.

"Thank you," Bianca says with a smile and a bat of her eyelashes. "I want to talk to you about something, but I need you to remember that it's my birthday and that I'm drunk."

Casey looks expectantly at Lea and me, and we both shrug at him. Lea chews her thumbnail.

"All right, I'll bite," he says to Bianca. He sits up straight, folds his hands on the bar, and makes a very serious face.

"Are you making fun of me?" she asks.

"Is that what you want to talk about?"

"No," she says, leaning back and crossing her arms.

"Maybe I'm making fun of you a little," he says.

I have to admit that I think Casey is cute. He's like a tall leprechaun, all freckles and red hair. I have no idea when that became my type.

"So, what did you want to talk about?" he asks.

"My friend Lea here," Bianca starts.

Lea puts her hand over her eyes and tries to pull Bianca away.

"No," Bianca says, smacking Lea's hand ineffectually. "Fine. I want to talk to you about your friend Gabe."

"Okay."

Lea looks like she might throw up.

"Is Gabe gay?"

"Wait, what?"

"Gabe. Is he a homosexual?"

"Not that I know of," Casey says with a smirk. "I'm pretty sure he's straight."

"Like how sure?"

"Like he talks about . . . girls." Casey's eyes flick to Lea for a fraction of a second.

"All right," Bianca says. "Fair enough. Thank you for participating in this random survey." Then she bows low and walks back to our booth.

Casey shakes his head and looks between Lea and me.

"I'm Lea and this is Maribel. Though I suppose you kind of already know that. Why am I so awkward?" she asks, turning toward me. I shrug.

Casey ignores her awkwardness and shakes our hands like nothing's weird. And like our super-drunk friend didn't just ask him if his friend was gay.

"It's nice to meet both of you officially. I'll see you around?" he asks as he pulls on his coat.

"Yeah, sure," I say. I am so lame.

"You guys come to parties at my house, right?"

"Yeah, Maribel knows a guy who knows a guy," Lea says. In fact, her voice is so flirtatious I feel this creeping sense of jealousy at her ease around Casey. I swallow it down.

"Well, we could exchange numbers? Cut out the middle man?" He says this directly to me and I'm so busy swallowing my jealousy I almost miss the moment.

"Oh, sure!" I say, handing him my phone.

And within seconds we're back at the booth, numbers exchanged, and Bianca's giggling uncontrollably.

"What?"

"I'm totally not that drunk," she says. "But I figured if I could put on a good show, we might just get the information we've been looking for."

Lea shakes her head. "You're kind of an evil genius."

JANUARY

Casey *(Gabe's friend)*

"Casey?"

"Gabe!"

"Why are you calling me?" he asks. I think I woke him up.

"Because I'm away at my grandma's for another couple of days but I have something very important to tell you and every text I composed just didn't come out right."

"Okay . . ." he says, his voice more awake now, but a lot more cautious.

"So, I saw Lea and all of her friends at the bar the last night of the semester."

"All right."

"One of them, Bianca, she was like out-of-her-mind drunk. And Lea and her roommate, Maribel, were obviously trying to keep her in check."

"I feel like this is a horror story. That's how scared I am right now."

"Don't be scared!"

"That doesn't help."

"It was just one little thing. Bianca asked if you were gay." I say it fast, like ripping off a Band-Aid.

"Oh," he breathes. "Oh. Really?"

"Yeah."

"Huh."

"Are you okay over there?" I ask after a long minute.

"I'm fine. This explains a lot."

"Such as?"

"Well, Lea usually seems mostly happy to see me. And then we'll start to talk or whatever and she gets sort of sad looking, like she remembers some unpleasant fact. And I kept thinking it was something I wrote she didn't like, or I don't even know. Something she heard about me. So it would make sense if she thought I was gay."

"I made sure to tell her you're not gay."

"Thanks. I mean, I'm not offended."

"Good."

"This just makes so much sense!" he cries, his voice lighter and happier.

"Glad I could help."

"I'm gonna go now. Because I detest talking on the phone. But good work, Casey."

"Thanks, man. I try."

Danny (Lea's friend)

Lea has requested to meet up with me during winter break. This isn't odd. Lea and I used to hang out all the time. What was odd was the formal nature of her text message.

At her request, I meet her at the diner in our hometown at noon on the Monday after New Year's.

"Hello, Daniel," she says, already seated in a booth.

"Hello, Azalea." I fold my hands, mirroring her serious posture.

"I've taken the liberty of ordering you disco fries because I have some bad news."

"What?"

"Gabe Cabrera is not a homosexual."

"Oh no," I say.

She nods. "Oh yes."

I put my head in my hands. I know I'm being dramatic, in part because I really am sad about this, but mostly to go along with Lea's dramatic reveal.

She pats my hand.

I sit up. "So, you gonna go for it?"

"Yes."

"Awesome. He's the most amazing and perfect and precious boy on the planet and you need to be with him if I can't."

"Thanks, Danny."

"So how did you find out?"

"Bianca pretended to be drunk on the last night of the semester and she stumbled up to his friend Casey and just flat out asked if Gabe liked girls."

I shake my head. "Genius. You girls are geniuses."

"I'd like to tell you I was in on the plan. I'm not sure Bianca was even in on her own plan until it was actually happening. I mean, there's no way she knew that Casey would be alone at that bar at that particular time."

I nod and then a thought hits me. "I take it the IDs worked well?"

"They did! Though I don't know, I feel like something gets lost in translation by not waiting until you're twenty-one." She shrugs. "I'm not sure how often I'll use mine."

"You know, that makes a lot of sense to me."

Two plates of disco fries are served and we dig in.

"I am sorry about Gabe," she says.

"It's not your fault he likes girls. It's not like you're so amazing you turned him straight or something."

She laughs.

"I really thought he was gay though. I had no idea I could be so off. Maybe he's a little bi? Or pansexual?"

"Probably not," she says, smiling.

"Bi-curious? Maybe a little?"

"I'll try to find out for you," she promises, patting my hand.

"And I'll help you woo him," I say with a wink.

Sam (Gabe's brother)

Gabe's sitting on a bench outside the library when I come out of work the first day everyone's back on campus for the spring semester. I'm going to miss the quiet of winter break.

"Hey," I say, kicking the bottom of his sneaker when he doesn't look up from his book.

"Oh, hi."

"What's up?"

"You wanna go to the dining hall with me?"

"I can't, I have a baseball meeting."

"Never thought I'd be jealous of a baseball meeting. Guess everyone else is busy, too, then."

"Yeah, but I'll walk with you in that direction?"

"Sure."

"Is that why you were stalking me? Because you didn't want to eat dinner alone?"

He shrugs. "Mom said you were working. Figured it couldn't hurt."

"Sorry about that."

"No big deal. I guess I just got used to being home over

break. And my dorm room is tiny and quiet and . . ." He trails off and shakes his head. "I don't know. It's dumb."

I bump our shoulders together. "It's not dumb. You just really love your big brother."

"Sure, something like that."

We meander in silence for a few minutes, people walking fast all around us, probably because it's brutally cold outside. But Gabe's taking his time.

"Do you know of anyone who's hiring?"

"You need money?" I ask.

"Of course I need money. I mean, the advisor position is great because it gives me a place to live, but there's no cash involved. I pretty much live on dining hall meals and Starbucks gift cards from Aunt Kate."

"What's the deal with those? Why does she think we like Starbucks so much?"

"I don't know. But seeing as how I have no money they might come in handy. Like if I wanted to ask someone on a date, or something, I could at least take her to Starbucks."

"Are you going to ask Lea out?"

"I don't know. I don't know how realistic that idea is. But it's something I think about."

"So," I say. "You know, if you need money, I think the library's hiring. It's clean, climate controlled, you never smell like grease or old milk."

"You do make it sound kind of wonderful."

"And if I tell them my brother needs a job, they'll take you."

"Cool."

I want to say more, because there's always more to say, but I leave it at that. I don't want to scare him off. He'd been doing well over break, seemed happy and more like himself than he has in a long time. I think my parents were relieved to just see him acting like Gabe.

"Everything else okay?" I ask.

"Yeah, it's good," he says. "Beginning of the semester means that I'll have lots of kids coming to see me this week, worrying about their schedules and whether or not they're making the right choices."

"I don't remember caring about that stuff as a freshman."

"I think I just have some overachievers in my dorm."

"Here," I say, handing him a ten-dollar bill as I'm about to head into the building where my meeting is.

"No, it's cool."

"Take it, you can pay me back when you get a job."

He shakes his head.

"If you're sad and you have to eat alone, at least go get some decent food."

"All right, fine. But it's a loan."

"Oh, don't worry. I'll keep a tab."

He punches me in the arm but at least he laughs.

Maxine *(a waitress)*

Those two darlings are back, all by their lonesome this time. It seems kind of sad that they're sitting alone, but at least this time they smiled and waved at each other. I think the girl would have sat with him but she didn't notice he was here until I was bringing her food out.

I see her staring and since it's an oddly quiet Sunday evening I decide to meddle.

I say, "You could go sit by him."

"What if he doesn't want me to?"

I lean down to talk to her more quiet-like. "Well, what you could do is go to the restroom, and when you're passing the table, ask if he's waiting for anyone."

"Okay," she says, her eyes big.

"And if he says he isn't, ask if he wouldn't mind some company. I bet you he'll say yes to that. And if he says no . . ."

"I'll die of embarrassment."

"At least you'll die knowing."

"He's really shy," she tells me.

"All the more reason to take the bull by the horns."

"He looks busy."

"He's flipping through a magazine, sugar," I say. "Listen, why are you here alone?"

"I was hungry and my roommate isn't back on campus yet and I didn't feel like finding any of my other friends."

"Maybe that's why he's here alone. And then next time,

you won't have to come here alone, you know?"

She nods and takes a deep breath before she stands up.

I stand behind the counter, making myself look useful as I wipe it down.

"Hi, Gabe," she says.

He smiles and nods. Oh, he is a shy one.

"Are you waiting for someone?"

He shakes his head and blushes.

"You maybe want some company?"

"All right," he says.

"I'm just gonna go get my food and come back?" she says.

"Okay."

"You don't mind?"

I kind of want to wring her neck. He's not giving her the response she wants, obviously, but he's also not saying no, he's not making up excuses. She's one of those girls who's so blinded by how much she likes this boy, she's ignoring his bashfulness.

He shakes his head and looks up at her.

She comes back with her cheeseburger platter and sits down, looking very uncomfortable.

"They have good burgers here," he says quietly.

"They do."

She sits and eats primly and I bring his grilled cheese out a couple minutes later.

"Look at you switching seats all over the place," I tease her.

I wish I could break the ice for them. I've never seen two kids look so scared of each other before.

He twists his fingers together and doesn't look at her. He so pointedly doesn't look at her that it's obvious to me at least that he's working hard not to look at her, like looking at her is going to mean she'll see on his face how much he likes her.

She smiles at me and I walk back behind the counter. It's quiet for a Sunday afternoon.

"Do you want to play hangman?" she asks, flipping over the placemat and grabbing a pen from her bag.

He nods and smiles and looks so relieved.

They play a few rounds and then she gets a text message.

"My roommate just got back, so . . . I gotta go," she says. "I'll see you around?"

He nods and waves and she's out the door in a whirlwind. He spends a good fifteen minutes writing something on the back of a placemat before crumpling it up and leaving. I can't stop myself from uncrumpling it and reading for myself.

Things I should have said but didn't:
1. *How are you?*
2. *How was your break?*
3. *Are you still taking creative writing part two this semester?*
4. *I like girls, just for the record.*

5. *I'm kind of an idiot and I don't know what to talk about.*
6. *Thanks for sitting with me.*
7. *Thanks for playing hangman.*
8. *We should do this again sometime. I could give you my number and then next time you could text me or something. Or I could text you. We could text each other and I would stop being so stupid and pathetic and talk to you even though I always feel pretty stupid and pathetic. And there's a lot of stuff I should tell you, because you might not like me as much if you know the other stuff, but maybe you still would.*
9. *I really like Buffy the Vampire Slayer.*
10. *Bye. (I didn't even say good-bye. Why do I suck so much?)*

I have to force myself to crumple it back up and throw it away. Because what I want to do is save it for that girl, so she knows how much of an effect she has on this boy.

Maribel *(Lea's roommate)*

"The most amazing thing just happened!" Lea says when she bursts into our dorm room.

"What?"

"I sat with Gabe at the diner and we ate food and played hangman!"

"That sounds like you babysat him."

She slumps onto her bed and makes an angry face.

"No! I mean, that's cute! Don't be angry!"

She toes off her shoes and throws one at me, missing by a mile, but I laugh and continue putting my clothes away. "Tell me exactly what happened and leave nothing out."

"Well, I think that old lady waitress at the diner—"

"Maxine?"

"Yes!"

"I love Maxine."

"Me too! I think she wants Gabe and me to like . . . hook up. She was giving me all this advice about sitting with him and then she was watching and smiling as we sat together."

I think about that for a second. "That's weird, but good. It means that other people see the chemistry the two of you have."

"I agree," Lea says. "He was friendly, but quiet, of course. So we played hangman when it became apparent that he wasn't going to exactly jump into small talk with me."

"I think that's sort of brilliant. Keep him engaged, show him you accept him. Good work."

"Thank you, ma'am."

I slump onto the floor. "What else?"

"Well, then you called so I left."

"You left?"

"Yes. I mean, I was done eating. It was weird, it would have been weird to stay longer."

I slap my forehead.

"Oh, don't be so dramatic," she says.

"No, but you should have stayed! You could have walked back together. Why would you leave? Right when things were sort of happening?"

"I don't know!" she says, throwing up her arms in exasperation. "Because I need you to be my life and relationship coach. I need to get a Bluetooth headset for you to whisper into and tell me when I'm making a mistake."

I narrow my eyes at her. "So I'll be outside hiding in the bushes or something?"

"Basically."

"We'll work on that plan."

Casey (Gabe's friend)

"What does it mean that Bianca asked you if I was gay?" Gabe asks the second I open the front door for him. He said he'd be over as soon as he finished eating. But that was literally like four minutes ago.

"How did you get here so fast?" I ask as he comes in and we head upstairs.

"Flying car."

"You don't drive," I toss back as we take seats in front of the TV and Gabe fires up the Xbox.

He side-eyes me and then takes a deep breath. "It means something, right?"

I accept his obvious subject change. "This means they talk about you."

"It does, right?" he says, licking his lips. "That's what I was thinking, but I wasn't sure if I was kidding myself or something."

"No way, they so obviously talk about you. Bianca and Lea and Maribel. Did I mention she did that thing where she introduced herself halfway through the conversation?"

"She's so cute," Gabe says, shaking his head. "She's never going to like me. I was just at the diner with her and we were sitting together—"

"Whoa, whoa, whoa. Back it up!"

"I know, I should have mentioned that sooner even though I've only been talking to you for fifty-three seconds."

"Damn straight."

"But like, I didn't say anything. We sat together for at least twenty minutes. I barely said two words. It was like I couldn't think of any words. Now I can think of about nine million words."

"How many words are in the English language?"

"Not the point."

"Sorry, you're right." I make a mental note to Google the number of words in the English language later on. "You can do this. I mean, you're gonna see her in class and she comes to parties here. . . ."

"But how do you go from like not really even being friends to dating?"

"Talk to her."

"Oh, yeah, 'cause that's easy."

"Dude, it's not like you don't have anything in common. Chat her up in class."

"Chat her up in class?" he asks, his voice robotic, mocking me. "Does not compute."

"You know, people are always like, 'Oh, that Gabe, he's so nice.' And I'm like, 'No, he's not. He's a dick to me.'"

"I have to get my dickish nature out somehow."

"Anyway. We'll figure this out with Lea. We have a whole semester to wrap this up. There's no way that she doesn't like you. She acts like she likes you. You told me that she even asked you to go out that one night. Girls don't do stuff like that if they don't like you."

"But what if she asked me because she feels bad for me or something?"

"Why would she feel bad for you?"

"I dunno, I guess she wouldn't." He stares at the ground.

"She doesn't know anything," I say, hesitant, treading lightly around the unspoken topic.

"I know. You're right."

"'Course I'm right. I'm your Yoda."

"Yeah, you're really not."

Inga (creative writing professor)

"Ready for another semester of fun?" I ask Cole as he comes into my office the day before our first class of the new semester.

"Oh, for sure."

"Let's get the boring stuff out of the way, and then we can gossip?" I suggest.

We talk for about a half hour about dividing up grading and confirming office hours. I give him a thorough description of my vision for the course, about how it'll be a lot more like a workshop with short assignments each class period and a lot more peer critiquing.

"Sounds good," he says, like he always does. He's without a doubt the best TA I've ever had.

"So how was your break?" I ask.

"It was good. My girlfriend and I went up to Boston for New Year's to see some of her friends. How was yours?"

"Fine," I say, and then I break into a grin. "I can't keep my mouth shut anymore. Look who both signed up for this semester?" I turn the roster to face him.

"Oh! Gabe and Lea!"

"This semester, Cole. They will get together. I don't care what I have to do, or who I have to take out in the process."

"I notice that Hillary is also on that list."

"I know, I've been trying to ignore her."

"I'm a little surprised she wanted to take part two."

"Believe me when I say I tried to talk her out of it. But there was no convincing her otherwise. I think my protestations actually spurred her on."

"Such a shame. Although, Inga," he says, and I know he's about to play devil's advocate, "she is a decent writer."

"For a bubblehead," I say, not wanting to relent.

"For a bubblehead," he agrees.

Victor (creative writing classmate)

When my friends asked me to go see a local band at a bar two towns over, they failed to mention it was an all-ages show. And that somehow this local band has garnered a ton of sixteen-year-old screaming girls as fans.

And worst of all, that Big Foot and the Giraffe are also fans of said band.

I don't know that they see each other right away, which is so freaking annoying because they should be together. They obviously deserve each other. If I tried to instill anything into those two in the four months that I was forced to be in their presence in class it was that they need to get their shit together and start dating. I mean, I don't really care, but this crap is annoying.

I do my best to ignore them, hitting on this chick Lilla who my friends insist likes me even though every time I try to talk to her, she just laughs at me and walks away. Even when

I'm not saying anything particularly funny.

About midway through the set, I go up to the bar. They're not serving much of anything, no liquor or mixed drinks, but at least they have beer on tap. I'm not picky as long as it's cold.

Just my luck though, I end up in line behind my archnemeses.

"That's six bucks," the bartender says to Big Foot.

"For a bottle of water?"

"Oh, I rang you and your girlfriend up together," the guy says, gesturing toward the Giraffe. Even in the dim light I can see the Giraffe blush.

"Oh." Big Foot starts digging deeper into his pockets and the Giraffe steps in.

"It's cool," she says. "I've got it."

"You don't . . ." Big Foot starts.

"I don't mind," the Giraffe says, smiling at him. "You can pay me back or something."

I want to smack their foreheads together. Maybe that will wake them up. How can they both be so blind?

She pays and then hands him the overpriced bottle of water.

"You didn't have to do that," Big Foot mumbles.

"Or you could just say thank you," Lea says, her face kind even if her words have a hint of snark to them.

"Thank you."

"You're welcome." She turns and walks away.

Big Foot turns toward me, giving me a dirty look

and pushing his way back to his friends.

At least he didn't want to fight.

There's no way I could have absorbed a kick from one of his massive feet.

Maribel (Lea's roommate)

"Where the heck have you been?" I shout at Lea as she moves back onto the dance floor with Bianca and me.

She holds up a bottle of water.

"Bless you!" I say, grabbing for it and taking a sip. "Oh, sweet relief!"

As the song winds down, Lea pulls Bianca and me off to the side.

"Gabe is here!" she says.

"You don't look very happy about that!" Bianca says.

"I'd be happier if he wasn't such a . . . buttprint sometimes!"

"What's a buttprint?" Bianca asks.

"Like a butthead but worse," Lea says, crossing her arms.

"Why is he a buttprint?" I ask.

"The bartender accidentally rang our waters up together so I bought them and it was like he didn't even want to thank me."

Bianca nods. "You stole his manhood!"

"I did not! He was digging in his pockets. I had a ten out

to pay. Let me pay, you buttprint."

"Stop being a buttprint!" I yell in his direction.

That makes her laugh.

"I know he's not going to automatically be in love with me. But like, he could have been nice to me. I don't need profuse joy for the sake of a bottle of water, but he was so vehement that I didn't need to pay. . . ."

"Lea, my love, my roommate, my special friend," I say, putting my hands on her shoulders. "You need to calm down. You're doing a really good job getting yourself out of your comfort zone when it comes to this guy, doing what you can. And I think it's going very well, and if he doesn't like you, screw him!"

"Thank you."

"Because you're being super sweet to this kid, and he's being mostly . . ."

"Aloof?" she offers.

"Yes, aloof."

"I know, but I feel like that's just him, like that's not about me. That's just how he acts."

"And," Bianca adds, "we have the proof thanks to his essay about being shy."

"I think I need to continue to forge ahead."

"Oh, I wasn't telling you to quit, I was just putting things into perspective."

She hugs me and we return to the dance floor.

Casey (Gabe's friend)

Gabe sits with his shoulders slumped for about fifteen minutes after he comes back from getting a bottle of water. I can't take it anymore.

"What's the deal?"

"Huh?" he says, squinting his eyes at me.

"What's wrong?" I yell, directly into his ear.

"Oh, Lea. She bought me this," he says, gesturing with his now-empty water bottle.

"Awesome!"

"Not really. It was only because she felt bad for me. The bartender rang us up together, but I didn't have enough money to pay for both. And I guess she saw me digging around in my pockets and I just looked so totally lame."

"So pay next time. You've got that sweet job at the library now."

"What next time? There's no point."

I give him a withering look and then he proceeds to pout for another half hour.

When I notice that Lea and her friends are on their way out, I gesture for him to go talk to her and he shakes his head. I grab his arm and race to cut them off before they exit.

"Tell her you'll get her next time," I say.

"I'll get you next time!" he yells as I push him within Lea's earshot.

She gives him a confused look as the three girls walk out the door into a gust of cold air.

"I sounded like a cartoon villain. She should be afraid of me."

"I didn't mean you should quote me word for word."

"I told you I suck at this."

"I should have listened."

Squirrel!

The boy passes first, but I'm too hungry to follow him.

Then the girl is on the green, so I sit up, hoping she'll notice me and stop and talk. And give me food.

I can't find my acorns again and it's going to snow soon.

Then I'll never find my acorns.

"Hey, little guy," she says when she sees me.

I stop and sit up straight, making my tail fluffy, and I blink at her.

"I don't have any food today."

She frowns at me.

"You're looking awfully skinny."

I try to frown at her.

"I'll bring food for you next time. I promise."

Luckily I get distracted from my hunger when a leaf cartwheels by on a stiff breeze. I decide to chase it.

Charlotte (a barista)

It's been a while since I've seen Gabe and Lea in here, though that's not particularly rare considering the time of year. But I'm almost happy when I see Gabe wander in Tuesday afternoon. He orders a coffee and settles down with his homework. About ten minutes later, Lea comes through the door, bright eyed and graceful and making me hate her and wish I was more like her at the same time.

"Hello," I say as she approaches the counter.

"Hi," Lea says. She seems so happy and I don't think she's even noticed Gabe yet. And as if he could hear me think about him, he appears next to her.

"Hi," he says to her.

She looks flustered. "Hey."

"This one's on me," he says.

"Oh, you really don't have to."

"No, I want to," he says, taking a deep breath. "I'm pretty sure I made a creepy cartoon villain promise while I was drunk the other night."

"It was a little bit like a cartoon villain."

I'm stunned by what I'm seeing. Something has definitely happened between them in the past month. Because the last time I saw them in here together, they barely even greeted each other, and now here Gabe is, buying her a drink. I can't wait for Keith to come back from his break. He's going to be so jealous he missed it!

"I didn't buy you a drink to get a drink back," she says. "It just happened."

"Then why did you say . . ." He trails off, shaking his head. "Listen, my aunt always gives me Starbucks gift cards for like every occasion. She gave me a fifty-dollar one for Christmas. She has stock in this place or something, I swear. So let me buy you a drink."

Her jaw drops. "That's the most I've ever heard you talk except for in class."

This is quite obviously the wrong thing for her to say, because he clamps his mouth shut and blushes furiously right to the tips of his ears. His shoulders tense up and his eyes sweep around the room. This conversation went from fun to something that I don't know if I can continue watching in about three seconds flat. The secondhand humiliation is palpable.

"I'm sorry," she says, putting a hand on his arm. "I didn't mean that in like a bad way. It's good, to hear you talk."

He heaves a long sigh and then rolls his eyes. "It's cool, I get that a lot. I'm not a big talker. Whatever."

"I'm starting to realize that."

"Lemme buy you a drink," he says, gesturing with an adorable tip of his head.

"All right." She turns to me, and it's weird because the tension that was there two seconds ago is magically gone simply because she relented. "I'll have a grande peppermint latte."

He stands with her while she waits for her drink and I

hear him say, "Do you want to, um, maybe, um, you can say no, of course. You could maybe, if you wanted to, sit with me." I hate to admit that it is absolutely endearing, the way he digs his hands so deep into his pockets and how he sort of kicks at the floor tile and doesn't look at her. I feel like this whole exchange is being wasted on me. I wish the others were here to see it.

It's a shame he's not looking at her though because the look of complete and utter delight on her face could kill puppies. She's like the happiest girl in the world, as if she's basically having the best day of her life.

"I'd like that," she says.

He looks at her then and smiles. "Yeah?"

"Yeah."

Keith comes back out front as Gabe and Lea sit down.

"Holy crap!" he exclaims. "They're sitting together!"

I laugh and tell him about what happened.

They sit there in the window of the coffee shop for almost an hour, not talking much, but looking at each other over the tops of their books, flirting somehow even without words.

It would be gross if it weren't adorable.

Bench (on the green)

No one sits on me all damn winter except that idiot squirrel. And now it's snowing and I'll be covered in the stuff for weeks and then I'll be all wet and I won't see a single butt for the whole duration.

All those ungrateful delinquents walk by hour after hour, day after day, week after week. Not one glance my way, not one single decent sitter in the whole bunch.

No one has time for benches in the winter.

If I could, I would grow spikes. That would show them, come spring when the birds are chirping and the sun is out. They would sit down and I would grow a spike right into their rotund rear ends. Then they'd stop taking me for granted.

FEBRUARY

Pam (Inga's wife)

Inga eyes me suspiciously when she catches sight of me through the window in the classroom door. She waves me in.

"Hey," she says, walking toward me, looking vaguely alarmed. "Is everything okay?"

"Yeah, I was going to wait outside, see if you wanted to go to lunch." I look around the classroom. There's a low hum of chatter going on as the students work together. I can see why Inga likes this group so much.

"And maybe spy on my couple?" she whispers between her teeth.

"Yeah, maybe that, too."

She makes a silly face. "I'm sure you can pick them out."

I take a good look around the room and she's right, it's easy to pick them out after all I've heard about them. Their desks are pushed close and their voices are quieter than the other groups around them, but their body language speaks volumes.

I can see why Inga was pulled to them.

"How many syllables in 'smile'?" one of the kids asks.

"They're working on a haiku project," Inga explains.

I watch Gabe and Lea for a few minutes before Inga dismisses the class.

"They're fascinating," I say as the door closes.

"They are. She's really come around to making him laugh and he just lights up anytime she says anything."

"Finally," I say.

"Finally," she agrees.

Bob *(a bus driver)*

I'm sitting outside the student center on my break when I see my two favorite kids. They don't seem to take the bus at all lately while I'm driving so it's nice to see them out and about. The girl walks out the door as the boy walks in.

"Hi, Gabe," she says.

"Lea," he responds.

I'm happy to know their names now, it'll make telling my

Margie about them a lot more fun.

They stop in the middle of all the students flowing in and out of the doors and just look at each other.

"Did you . . ." she starts to say, as he starts to say, "Can I . . ."

I'll never know what they were about to say, because someone bumps into him from the side at that moment and they both seem to lose their train of thought.

"I guess I should . . ." he says, gesturing in the other direction.

She nods and tips her head toward the entrance to the student center.

They definitely remind me of Margie and me except for three differences. We met at a go-go bar, we're not particularly educated, and she's not Asian. But if it weren't for those things, they'd be just like us. I told her about them and now she likes when I tell her stories. Sometimes I make stuff up since I haven't seen them in a while.

But now I can tell her I saw them, and about how they were happy to see each other, bashful and awkward, but happy. It's like our own little soap opera that no one else knows about.

They're gone now, both out of sight, so I go back to reading my paper and freezing out here. But I always need some fresh air after being cooped up on the bus so much.

I see we're supposed to have a big snow later on this week,

biggest in years they're saying. Hopefully they close the school because I hate driving in that garbage. Call me a bad driver, call me a fraidy cat, but no one should be on the roads when the weather's bad.

Casey (Gabe's friend)

I sneak onto the elevator in Gabe's lobby without calling first and hit the button for the ninth floor. I head down the hallway and knock on his door, hoping he's around.

"Hey," he says when he opens the door.

"It's snowing."

"I know."

"We're all gonna go play football or some shit and I came over here specifically to drag your ass out."

He pulls up his left sleeve and shows me some gauze wrapped around his elbow.

"What happened?"

"I got the pins out over the weekend. Do you listen to anything I say?"

"I guess not," I admit. "So that means you can't come out at all?"

He rolls his eyes. "I probably could come out, but I shouldn't exactly play tackle football with stitches in my throwing arm."

"So you could cheerlead. I hear that Lea might be around," I tell him.

He perks up at that, but then frowns. "Let me go find some layers."

I step into his tiny room. It's basically built for a monk and barely big enough for the school-issued bed, desk, and dresser. I look at the pictures he has tacked onto his corkboard while he changes.

When he's ready to go, he has on track pants and his high school baseball sweatshirt.

"I've got layers upon layers and I put a little extra padding around my elbow."

"Where are you living next year? Have you thought about it?" I ask.

He shrugs, tugging his ski jacket on. "I could do this again maybe. I don't know that I'm exactly excelling at it, but it was nice of the school to find a way to make up for some of the scholarship I lost. And I'm actually kind of good at it."

"If that doesn't work out, I bet somebody will move out of our house. You could move in with me and Sam."

"You're staying around here after graduation?"

"I don't know, probably. We'll keep you posted."

"Costs a lot of money," he mutters.

"You're too young to worry so much about money."

Gabe laughs as he pulls his gloves on and shoves a hat in his pocket.

"All right, let's go."

"I'm sorry I forgot about your elbow stuff," I say when we're in the elevator.

"No big deal."

"Does it hurt, right now?"

He shrugs. "Not bad like it did after it happened. Mostly the cuts hurt from where they took the pins out."

"I feel like an asshole for not remembering."

"I don't ever really say much about that stuff." He starts to whistle tunelessly and I take that as a hint to move past this topic.

We walk outside and even though it's two in the afternoon there's a weird quality outside like it's almost dusk.

"Usually snow makes everything seem too bright," he says, looking around as we walk.

"I think it's because the clouds are so dense or something."

"Thank you, Al Roker."

"That's funny you bring him up. He's the one who told me the clouds would be particularly dense during this storm."

"I think you missed your calling as a meteorologist."

The walk to the green takes ten times longer than usual because the snow is at least eight inches deep.

"So what's up with Lea?" I ask.

"Not much."

"Are you going to like . . . ask her out or something?"

"I don't know how to do that."

"You say, 'Hey, Lea, let's go out sometime.'"

"I don't have a car."

"So?"

"It's not like I could take her to the movies."

"Think outside the box a little, Gabe. You're so full of self-doubt. Don't do that to yourself."

"We'll see what happens if she's here today."

We come out on the green and there's already a group of people there, including Bailey and a bunch of my roommates. He jogs over to us.

"You ready for some football?" he asks.

"We forgot about his bum elbow," I tell Bailey, gesturing toward Gabe.

"Oh, man." Bailey slaps his forehead. "What are you doing here? We should put you in bubble wrap and send you to bed."

"You sound like my mom."

"Yes, I'd imagine that Mrs. Cabrera would be a big proponent of that idea."

Gabe rolls his eyes. "Well, I'm here because maybe . . ." He glances around and he smiles before he even finishes that thought. Across the green are Lea and her friends, picking their way toward us.

"Bailey set that up for you. He got Bianca's number a couple of weeks ago," I tell Gabe, patting him on the shoulder.

"I'm gonna freeze my balls off," Gabe grumbles.

"Lea will keep your balls warm," I say.

"Now go be a good cheerleader and sit on that bench," Bailey adds.

"The bench that's completely covered in snow?"

"Yes. Clean it off and maybe the girls will join you."

He groans but walks over there, pulling his hat onto his head and putting his hood back on before scooping the snow off the bench and plopping down.

"I feel kind of bad," Bailey says.

"He seems okay about it," I say, looking at Gabe thoughtfully. "Come on, let's get this going."

Sam trots over to us.

"Why didn't you tell us Gabe was getting the pins out of his elbow?"

He makes a face. "I totally forgot. I am the worst brother ever."

Bianca comes over by the boys and wants to play, but Maribel and Lea take a seat by Gabe. I'm happy to see Lea sitting right next to him. Unfortunately Gabe is sitting as far away from her as possible, basically hugging the arm of the bench.

I lose track of them during the game and eventually it seems like everyone is having a snowball fight rather than following any of the rules of football. I glance back over by the bench and Gabe is sitting by himself and apparently talking to a squirrel.

I'm a little bit concerned.

_____

Bench *(on the green)*

Well, well, well. Looks like someone's finally cleaning me off. Probably just gonna use the snow to make snowballs or a fort or something. But it's nice to feel the wind at least, sort of refreshing after weeks of being under ice.

What's this? Are they actually sitting down, too? And is it possible that this is my favorite butt from way back when? This day has gotten a lot better. Considering I thought it would be another in a long string of lonely days on this tundra.

He seems a little tense.

Oh, damn, it's because he seems to have some lady friends joining him. Terrible. And they're making the whole structure off balance and he's turned all wrong. Go away, ladies, you're ruining the perfect butt.

"Hey, Gabe," they both say with varying levels of enthusiasm. If you're going to talk to this great ass, at least be excited about it.

He doesn't say anything in return but I think he might at least wave or something.

"What's up?" one of the girls asks.

No response.

"Not a big football fan?" the other one asks.

I can feel him shrug, but I'd kind of like to tell him that he should probably talk. Unless he doesn't like these broads; maybe that's why he's so tense.

After what seems like a really long time, too long to wait to respond to a question, he says, "I hurt my elbow."

"Are you okay?" a girl asks, her voice worried.

He's slow to answer again. What's with this kid?

I hope the girls leave soon so he can relax and I can enjoy our time together.

Maribel (Lea's roommate)

Lea is working really hard to talk to Gabe and he's giving her nothing to work with. I'm starting to think he's a lot weirder than I realized. Either that or our voices are getting lost in the wind. I feel bad for Lea.

"Which assignment did you pick for class?"

He kind of scrunches up his face and shakes his head, but I'm not sure if that's answering Lea's question or whether he was trying to get the snowflake off his nose.

"So, you played baseball in high school?" she asks, pointing toward the sweatshirt underneath his unzipped coat. I should yell at him to zip it up; it's freezing out.

He crosses his arms and smiles at her.

"Yeah, I played softball," she mumbles.

I would think we were bothering him, but he looks at her a lot. It's like he's trying read her mind rather than hear what she's saying.

"It's cold," I say. "Come on, let's play."

She looks forlornly over at Gabe and then gestures to the group. "We're gonna go play."

He does an adorable tip of his imaginary hat brim, so at least I know he has some personality in there somewhere.

"That was painful," she mutters to me as we walk over to the group.

"I'm glad you noticed."

"I'm not delusional, Mar," she says. I just feel bad because on our way here she was so excited and bouncy, and now she's confused more than anything. The boy you like should never make you that confused.

I roll up a snowball and throw it at Casey. He looks at me with mock surprise and throws one back and then pauses, looking over my shoulder. I follow his eye and notice that Gabe looks sad and small and appears to be talking to a squirrel.

Squirrel!

It's been so long since anyone came and played on the green and all of these people are here and they're all playing and I wonder if they know where my acorns are.

I run in circles around them, careful not to get stepped on the way my friend did once. His tail has never been the same. After running up and down all the trees and watching them play for a long time, I notice one of them is sitting alone.

He likes the girl, I can tell. She was sitting by him before, but now she's gone and he looks sad.

I zigzag over toward him and hop up on the bench. I sit for a while. This is my favorite bench. I'm happy all these people are here, but I'm sad that this boy looks so sad.

"This sucks," he mutters.

Is he talking to me?!

I look up at him and he looks down at me.

"How's it going, little squirrel?"

I am overjoyed! Hooray! I've made another friend. Maybe he can help me locate my acorns!

"Are you the same one I always see Lea talking to?"

I fluff up my tail, hoping that's the response he's looking for.

"I bet it's not so bad being a squirrel. I bet you're cooler than I am. Like if the girl you liked spent a half hour sitting with you on a bench you would actually talk to her. But I couldn't really hear her through my hat, and my hood, and over the wind. And I wanted to switch sides, because that would have been easier, but her friend was over there and there was no way to do it without being conspicuous. And eventually I'm going to have to explain everything to her, but I don't want her to feel bad for me. And no matter what, I still don't like talking about it."

I turn my head to the side to really look at him. I don't

know what he's talking about, but he's obviously very sad about it. I try to think of some way to make him happy.

"You ready to go?" one of his friends asks. Or maybe it's his brother. They both kind of look the same. But the humans all kind of look the same to me.

"Yeah."

"Want to say good-bye to your new best friend the squirrel?"

"Hey, man. That squirrel's a good listener."

"I could be a good listener, too, if you gave me a chance."

Sam (Gabe's brother)

Gabe doesn't say anything for a few minutes and I feel suspiciously like we're in an after-school special.

"I know you'd listen."

"Well, that's something."

"I just don't have anything to say."

I nod. "You don't have to say anything important. I know everything has completely sucked for the past year and I'm sorry about that."

"Thanks."

We walk slowly back to my house. I'd told my roommates to go ahead and get pizza without us. Gabe obviously has something on his mind, so maybe he'll talk about it if it's just the two of us.

"I slept through a fire drill the other night."

"Seriously?"

"Yeah."

"How do you even do that?"

"I fell asleep on my good side with an earbud in."

"Dude."

"I know. It's obviously not a good situation. I don't think I realized how bad it was."

"You could like . . . die."

"I would hope that someone would realize I wasn't outside and they'd send firefighters in for me or something."

"Gabe, this is not the time to be glib."

"I'm not being glib. I'm trying to reassure myself."

I'm at a loss for anything to say.

"The flashing light did finally wake me up and I stumbled out the side fire exit as everyone was going back in."

"You should probably get that checked out."

"I'm definitely coming to terms with that fact."

"You hungry?"

"Of course."

We're about to turn onto my street but instead we walk in the direction of the sandwich place. The least I can do is buy the kid a meatball sub.

Before we walk in to order, he pulls me aside.

"I need to get everything right in my head. Sometimes I get sort of overwhelmed and confused. And then I feel.

It's a lot of . . . emotions. And I hate it."

I nod. Those are a lot of emotions.

"I'm still seeing that shrink, and it's getting better."

"Good."

"But today with Lea kind of sucked. It was like everything that I know is wrong became grossly apparent."

"She talked to you a lot."

"I couldn't hear anything she said."

"It really doesn't have to be like that."

"I want you to believe me when I tell you that I've come to that conclusion."

"Cool. Or else I'll have to pull some kind of big-brother advantage and make it happen."

He pushes me out of the way and walks through the door, pulling it shut behind him before I even know what hit me.

"You haven't had big-brother advantage since I got taller than you when we were in middle school," he mutters as I stand behind him in line.

I don't say anything.

"I'm going to take your silence as agreement," he says seriously.

I burst out laughing. I kind of lucked out in the younger-brother department.

———————

Danny (Lea's friend)

"He works at the library!" I say to Lea as I pull her in for a hug.

"Gabe?" she asks.

"Yes." I've come to terms with the fact that Gabe will never be mine, so I am going to do my damnedest to help Lea woo him. "Let's go stalk him."

I thread my arm through hers and we walk in the direction of the library.

"You don't seem particularly excited," I say as we get to the front doors.

"Things are sort of weird with him lately."

"Weird how?"

"Well, they were really good for a while. Like fun and normal and every time I saw him we would talk and even kind of hang out."

"But . . ."

"But then I saw him during the snowstorm and I was sitting on the bench by him because he hurt his elbow and he couldn't play snow football," she says.

"He hurt his elbow, so precious," I say, putting a hand to my heart.

She smiles. "I was talking to him, asking him a lot of questions, but like he never answered. He would sort of shrug or whatever but he never talked. I thought we were past that, you know?"

I make my most sympathetic face.

"Anyway, I hate to complain. Because he hasn't done anything wrong. But I also can't help but feel like he paid his debt to me that day in Starbucks and now he never wants to talk to me again." Her shoulders droop. We're standing near the elevator.

I put a finger under her chin and lift her face up. "Don't be so sad."

She pouts more dramatically and pushes my hand out of the way. I grab for her hand and pull her onto the elevator.

"We're going to find that boy and make him talk to you."

"That sounds awfully threatening," she says.

"Okay, so we'll stake out a table with a good view over by the balcony and you can watch him from afar."

"I like that idea a lot more."

We find a table that looks out into the tall atrium at the center of the building. We study for a while, goofing off and chatting more than really getting anything done. At one point, Lea looks down to the first floor and freezes.

"Look," she whispers.

And there's Gabe with a cart full of books. I can't help but check out the way his shoulder muscles move as he pushes.

"I guess his elbow still hurts," she says.

"He does seem to be favoring the one side."

Lea puts her chin in her hand, watching until he's out of sight.

"You like him a lot," I say.

"I do," she says. "But it's dumb. He's just not that into me. When you're into someone you don't sit next to them for thirty minutes in the freezing cold and barely say a word to them. You don't talk to them in class and then ignore them almost everywhere else."

I nod. She has a point.

"Let's get out of here," she says. "I feel pathetic stalking him."

As we're collecting our stuff, the elevator behind us dings and wouldn't you know, out pops Gabe.

Lea studies him for a moment and he waves. She takes a half step toward him and then slightly shakes her head.

She turns toward me and grabs my arm. "Let's go."

I'm quiet as we jog down the stairs and out of the building.

"What was that about?" I ask once we're outside.

"I don't know. I think I need to stop torturing myself with him."

"He obviously wanted to talk to you."

"Or maybe I would have done all the talking and he would have ignored me again. I don't like this game anymore."

I frown at her and then pull her toward the student center. "I think you need FroYo."

Casey *(Gabe's friend)*

"You look like someone killed your dog," I say to Gabe when he comes out of the library after his shift. We're meeting up to get dinner. He generously offered me the use of his meal plan.

"I kind of feel like someone killed my dog," he says, frowning as we head in the direction of the dining hall.

"You wanna talk about it?"

"Lea was at the library with some other guy," he says after what feels like a million years of silence.

"So?"

He shrugs. "So, she saw me and I waved and she turned away."

"Ouch," I say, instantly regretting it. I don't want to fall down this spiral with Gabe. "Maybe you should just ask her about the guy the next time you see her."

"I don't know. They seemed close. I didn't get a good look at him, but he like, touched her face and gave her a hug."

"That doesn't mean they're dating or something. They could be friends."

"I don't know, this felt like more than friends." He gives the dining hall worker his card and tells her he's using a guest meal, so she swipes it twice.

He doesn't say much as we get our dinner and locate a table and start eating.

"I was having a really good day," he tells me as he stabs at his chicken turnover.

"What's with the act of violence you're committing on that puff pastry?" I ask. He grimaces in response but ignores my comment.

"I woke up today in a good mood. I was feeling like I could do this. Like life isn't perfect and it even kind of sucks sometimes, obviously, but things could suck a lot worse. And I'm making money. I have friends, and I'm doing better in my classes this semester. I really like my job in the dorm even. Helping the first-years with their own stuff is really helping me."

I feel like texting Sam while Gabe is talking to let him know that Gabe is *talking*, saying meaningful things. I don't know what to say back though. I'm sort of terrible at emotional stuff.

"I don't mean to dump this all on you. I guess I finally could see something happening with Lea and me, and then there she was hanging out at the library, getting cuddly with some other guy."

"It sucks. If I could change it I totally would."

"Yeah, I know. I appreciate that. I just keep coming back to the fact that if something ever happens with her, I'm going to have to tell her all this sort of pathetic stuff about me."

"It's not pathetic."

He sighs. "I know. I guess I feel pathetic about it, and I don't want her to think I'm pathetic. . . . It's really complicated in my brain. I can't imagine telling her about what happened."

"Maybe you should try to start telling people? Other people? About what happened? Maybe that would desensitize you."

He gives me a questioning look.

"I'm taking abnormal psych this semester to meet girls."

"Then I should obviously take your advice."

"I'm just saying desensitization is a valid form of therapy."

He throws a pea at me.

MARCH

Squirrel!

"Hey," the boy says. "Are you the same squirrel I was talking to the other day? I wonder if you remember me. Do squirrels have memories?"

He tosses some breadcrumbs from his sandwich. I haven't had an acorn in weeks so his crumbs taste really good. I've had other food, but nothing as tasty as breadcrumbs.

"I was thinking about telling my professor something about me." He leans his elbows on his knees and then jerks back. "I keep forgetting about my elbow. Usually it just aches a little, but I had to get the pins out of it, so I can't really lean on it right now."

I stare at him.

"The thing is, it shouldn't be a big deal. I hate that I've made it this big deal in my head. People are in car accidents all the time."

I run up onto the bench to sit next to him.

"But I guess people don't always lose so much in them."

I twist my head to look at him and he leaves a few more crumbs on the bench.

"Or they lose a lot more than I did."

He stands up.

"All right, time to go talk to Inga. I think I'm ready."

He turns back to look at me.

"You really are a very good listener."

Pam (Inga's wife)

As I walk through the door that night, Inga immediately drags me into the living room, sits me on the couch, and hands me a glass of wine.

"I had a breakthrough with Gabe today," she says, her voice excited.

"You do realize that you're not actually his therapist," I say.

She gives me a withering look.

"Just checking."

The withering intensifies.

"I don't think I've ever seen you quite this invested in anyone."

"They're such nice kids," she says.

I nod and take a sip of my wine.

"Anyway, I just can't wait to tell you what happened. I almost called you at work."

I sit up straight, ready to listen.

"Anyway, he came to see me today at office hours," she says, her enthusiasm so tangible that it's catching. "And he asked me if I thought he was doing a good job in the class."

"And of course you think he is."

"Yes. He said his major is currently undeclared because of something that happened last year."

"What happened?" It's in this moment that I realize I'm almost as invested as she is.

"He was in a bad car accident. Apparently he lost his hearing in one ear and shattered his elbow."

I put my hand up to my mouth. "That's terrible!"

"It is. And the worst part is that he'll never play baseball again."

"He used to play baseball?"

"Yeah, he had a scholarship and everything."

I shake my head sadly. There's an injustice there that I can't quite put my finger on.

"He says he's getting help though; he's seeing a therapist because he's been having trouble coming to terms with some of the aftereffects, particularly the fact that his hearing loss is permanent."

"Poor kid."

"The good news is that the school gave him a position in one of the freshman dorms so he wouldn't have to pay for housing. So that's something at least."

"It can't be easy to deal with."

"I know, but it also explains a lot."

"It does. So he was wondering if I thought it would be worth it for him to major in English. We went through the whole thing about job opportunities and what he wants from life. Before the accident he was majoring in physical education because he figured he'd love to be a baseball coach. But now that's not in the cards for him."

"Must have been some accident if he can't play baseball anymore."

"I know. It just makes me so sad."

"Did he decide anything?"

"Well, it's funny. Because after we talked a little more, he started to think that maybe he'd like to be a counselor of some kind. He was telling me about the kids he works with in the dorms and how he really does enjoy it. It was nice to see him so animated about it."

"Sounds like a good day."

"It really was."

Casey (Gabe's friend)

"Hey!" I say, catching sight of Gabe coming out of a random office building the Monday after spring break. I jog to catch up with him.

"Hey!" I repeat, well aware that he didn't hear me, so I touch his arm.

"Oh, hey," he says, smiling.

"What are you doing down here?"

"Um, well, that's my therapist's office," he says, pointing vaguely.

"Oh." I feel like I don't know what else to say. "How's that going?"

He thinks for a minute. "It's going really well."

"Cool."

"What are you doing down here?" he asks.

"I needed a new parking permit, but there's not any good parking near the parking authority so I had to walk down and now I'm walking back."

He shakes his head and rolls his eyes. "Lack of parking at the parking authority. Sometimes this place is the worst."

"What are you doing right now?"

He flashes a gold Starbucks card.

"Aunt Kate strikes again?"

"The woman loves sending me Starbucks gift cards. I don't even enjoy their coffee that much. I don't like coffee that much period. But I suppose it's starting to grow on me. I've

♥ 167 ♥

also become kind of addicted to some of their pastries."

"Let's go," I say. It's a short walk and we're entering the coffee house in no time.

"Hey," Gabe says to the girl behind the counter as we step up to order. CHARLOTTE, her name tag reads. "Long time no see."

The girl rolls her eyes, but smiles. "I broke my foot when I slipped on some ice."

"Last year I was in a car accident and I shattered my elbow and lost all hearing in my left ear."

She blinks at him. "So it's a competition?"

Gabe laughs and I stand there stunned. I don't think I've ever seen him like this. I have to wonder if his therapist medicates him during their sessions. Or maybe he gets hypnotized and she forgot to snap him out of it. We collect our drinks and move toward an available table.

"I talked to my therapist about trying the desensitizing thing," he tells me before I can ask the obvious question.

"You know, I got that idea."

He chews his lip and thinks it over. "Okay. So, here's the deal," he says. "I've been thinking about this a lot lately, about my hearing. The doctor said maybe it would get better. Not like magically better, but you know, I'm young and it might improve. My other ear would start making up the difference or something. And I thought maybe I would get really good at lip reading but that has yet to happen. Instead

I spend a lot of time looking at people's mouths and getting nowhere."

I nod. "It would be cool if all your other senses would get better. Like Daredevil. How's your sense of smell, Gabe-o?"

"Daredevil's blind, you asshat."

"Still, it could happen."

"That's what I kept telling myself. Except now it's been over a year and it's really affecting my everyday life. It's making school harder and talking to people harder. I've never been good at talking to people to begin with, but when you can't hear them it's impossible."

"What do your parents think?"

He sighs. "I talked to them about it last time I was home. I think they were relieved that I finally admitted that things weren't great."

"So now what happens?"

"We made an appointment with an audiologist for over spring break. I don't know exactly how the timeline works, but it's a start."

I nod. "That sounds like a good idea."

"It costs a lot of money. So I feel guilty about that. Especially because they already took out a second mortgage to pay all of my hospital bills or whatever."

"Don't they have insurance?" I ask.

"Of course, but it turns out all that stuff costs a lot of money even with insurance."

I want to make sure I look as interested as I feel so that he keeps talking.

"So, how much does a hearing aid cost?" I ask.

"Like a thousand bucks, maybe more, depending on what I need. But I'm not sure a regular hearing aid would even really help me. There's this other kind of hearing aid where it transmits sound from your deaf side to the not-deaf side."

"You've been doing your research."

"Yeah, well, I work at a library now. I feel like I need to hone my skills."

"This all sounds suspiciously like good news."

"It is good news. It's pretty cool. There are these other wireless ones and teeny-tiny ones that you can barely see. But it's hard because I have to come to terms with this idea. This idea of needing a hearing aid."

"It's not a big deal."

"It's not. But it is. It's like I am a Deaf person. I have something wrong with me and people can see it and I can't hide it."

"And this is why you haven't wanted to talk about it," I say, light finally dawning in my idiotic brain.

"Yeah. I want stuff to be normal. But the more I try to make it normal, the worse I feel. And I have all this guilt, because I lived and I'm really fine. No one died. I'm not in a wheelchair, and I'm not blind. I'm a little bit deaf and I can't play baseball anymore. In the scheme of things, that's nothing."

"It's still a lot to deal with," I say.

"Thanks for saying that. Sometimes I think it is, and sometimes I feel like I'm being a baby about it. But it's good to hear someone else say it."

"Okay. So." I start ticking these issues off on my fingers. "We have the denial, the money, the guilt. Anything else?"

"Nope, that's basically it."

"You do realize, aside from a variety of other benefits, that if you have a hearing aid it will mean people can also see why you might not be responding. They wouldn't assume that you're ignoring them all the time."

"I hadn't thought about it like that."

"You should totally think about it like that," I say, leaning back in my chair. "And thank your aunt Kate for this rocking caramel macchiato next time you talk to her."

"Indeed I will."

"Well then, I declare this meeting of Gabe and Casey over."

Maribel (Lea's roommate)

When I get back from chem lab, there's a note on the whiteboard that apparently Bianca "misses my freaking face." I toss my things on my bed and then head upstairs to see what she's up to.

"Hey," I say as I approach her open door and knock on the doorjamb.

She smiles and slips off her earbuds before sitting up and bouncing on her bed. "I have good news!"

"What?"

"Bailey texted me to see what I was doing tonight."

"Yes! Progress."

"And I lied and said I was going to the movies with a friend."

"Why?"

"I don't know! I panicked. Since I didn't already have plans I didn't want to end up saying something stupid like that I was washing my hair."

"Fair enough," I say, taking a seat on her roommate's bed.

"So, he asked to come along."

"But you're not actually going to the movies."

She smiles a gigantic smile and I can tell I'm about to get roped into something. "Well, then he said he'd tag along with us, if that was okay. So, I'm going if you say you want to."

"Did you just trick me into going to the movies as a third wheel with you and Bailey?"

"He said he'll bring a friend."

"Do you think he'll bring Gabe?" I ask.

"I don't know. He didn't specify. Maybe we should bring Lea?"

"Danny picked her up to go home for spring break like ten minutes ago. I ran into them in the parking lot."

"Too bad."

"You think Gabe likes her?" I ask. The three of us spend so

much time together that it's rare that Bianca and I ever get a chance to speculate about Lea's crush on Gabe.

"I think they're pretty much in love but they're too stupid to do anything about it," Bianca says.

"Yeah, I have to agree," I say. "How are we getting to the movies?"

"Bailey said he'd pick me up at eight."

"All right. What'll we do until then?"

"Nap?"

"Always a solid idea."

Sam (Gabe's brother)

The dorms close for spring break, so I'm supposed to be on my way to take Gabe home as requested by our mother. But he insisted that we stop at the convenience store by his building because he was craving a Twix bar and root beer.

"Why does it have to be that particular combination?" I ask.

"Don't knock it til you've tried it," he insists.

My buddy Antonio is working the register so I stop to chat with him about the calc midterm we took the other day.

"It was the worst," I say.

"It was challenging," he says. But he's not paying attention to me. At some point in our conversation, Lea walked in and I didn't even notice. He's watching her and my brother walk around the store.

"Watch these two," he says.

"Why?"

"'Cause they come in here every once in a while, and she goes to one corner and he goes to the other, and then they move around the store creating parabolas as they come together and bounce apart. They're the weirdest couple on Earth. I want to write math equations about them."

I give him what I hope is my most confused look. "I think you've been spending too much time with your stats textbook."

"No, really, look. Their trajectory of attraction is like an equation."

He brings out a piece of paper and starts drawing graphs and writing long lines of numbers. He talks while he works, and soon Gabe and Lea are standing there watching him, too.

When he realizes he has an audience, he pauses his pencil. "You know we're running a deal on the giant bag of Twix if you want to share."

Lea and Gabe look at him blankly.

"Aren't you together?"

"Together?" Lea asks.

"Yeah."

She shoots a glance at my brother. "We're not together."

"But statistically . . . it would seem like you're attracted to each other."

"This is the weirdest conversation I've ever had," I tell Antonio.

"This happens to us a lot," Gabe says. I keep myself from celebrating that he actually spoke in front of Lea.

Antonio shrugs and rings up Lea's purchases. "It's true, the math is solid."

"Lea my love," a guy says from the doorway. "The natives are getting restless."

She giggles. "I assume by 'natives' you mean . . . you?"

"I mean all the parents picking up their kids who want my parking spot."

"All right," Lea says.

She smiles at us and leaves.

"You saw that, right?" Gabe says to me.

"Yes."

"And you heard what he said."

"Yes."

Antonio shakes his head. "It makes no sense. By my calculations, you're perfect for each other."

Danny (Lea's friend)

"So that was weird," Lea says as we head toward my car.

"First, the matter at hand," I say. "Did you get me my Twix bar?"

She hands me a bag.

"Thanks, sugar. So, what was going on in there?"

"The guy who works in the store told me and Gabe that he

could predict our level of attraction to each other by charting our trajectories and the fact that we made a parabola in the store as we were shopping for snacks."

I stare at her.

"I know," she says.

"Interesting," I say. "I wonder if that theory would hold any water. I feel like we could make millions writing some kind of self-help book involving math and romance."

"Yes, Danny. That's definitely the takeaway from what just happened in there."

We pull away from the curb and she sighs, checking her phone.

"Great, Maribel and Bianca are going out with Gabe's friends tonight. I can just imagine what they're going to talk about."

I make a noise that I hope is completely noncommittal.

She rolls her eyes. "And what if Gabe's there. I need to make them swear not to talk about me." She types furiously into her phone.

"Maybe it would help. . . ."

"I don't know. I'm tired of it. I'm really tired of being embarrassed all the time. And trying and having nothing happen."

"At least you're trying," I say. I hate not having any advice for her. I love giving advice and this whole situation makes me feel kind of useless.

"Ugh," she groans, putting her face in her hands. "When did I become so self-absorbed?"

"I promise you're not self-absorbed. You're wonderful. Everyone loves you. Including your friends. And if they talk about you with Gabe's friends, they won't say anything bad."

"I know, I know. You're right." She puts her phone in the cup holder.

"Good girl."

Casey (Gabe's friend)

"So, Gabe just flat-out refused to go?" Bailey asks as we drive across campus.

"Yeah, I texted him even though I knew Sam already left to pick him up to take him home for break. I thought maybe the lure of hanging out with Lea would be enough to get him to stay tonight."

"And you told him that we were going out with Bianca and her friend?"

"Yes."

"And that her friend might be Lea?"

"Well, he said that there was no way it could be Lea because she's running around campus with her boyfriend."

"Are we sure Lea has a boyfriend?"

"He seemed sure," I say. "He has an appointment with an audiologist tomorrow—"

"For like his ear stuff?"

"Yes."

"Oh, yeah, that's a good thing."

"And that he kind of doesn't want to do anything about Lea until he has that settled. But he was really bummed that she was with that guy again."

We pull up outside the dorm and Bianca and Maribel are waiting outside. Before they get in, I turn to Bailey.

"We should try really hard not to talk about Gabe and Lea."

"All right. I'll do my best."

The girls slide into the backseat.

"Hello, ladies," I say.

After everyone exchanges pleasantries we're quiet for what feels like an hour but in reality is three minutes, tops.

"Okay," Bailey says, turning to look in the backseat as we're stopped at a red light. "I'm going to address the elephant in the car."

"Bailey," I say, hoping my voice holds the same note of warning my mom's did that time I told my aunt her hair was aviation orange.

"Lea and Gabe. What's the deal?"

"I don't know if we should talk about it. . . ." I say.

But Maribel starts talking anyway. "I don't know how much we should say, but those two seriously need to get their acts together. I mean, how can it be so obvious to everyone around them and not to them?"

"You know the diner waitress?" Bianca says.

"Maxine?" I ask.

"Yes. She loves them. We were in there the other day and she asked Lea how her 'fella' was doing."

"Yeah, she does that with Gabe, too," Bailey says. "Except she calls Lea his 'sweetheart.'"

"Did you guys hear about the Chinese-food delivery guy?" Maribel asks.

"Oh, for sure. A word-for-word account."

"Does Lea have a boyfriend?" Bailey asks.

"Um, no."

"Gabe says he sees her around with some guy."

The girls give each other a look. "Not unless you mean Danny," Maribel says.

Bailey and I shrug. "We don't know his name," I say, flicking my eyes to the rearview mirror.

"Danny's her friend from high school," Maribel says.

"He is a boy who is her friend, but *definitely* not her boyfriend," Bianca adds.

"That could be the guy," Bailey says.

"So what are we going to do?" Bianca asks, getting down to business.

"Gabe has . . ." I pause, and Bailey and I exchange our own look. "Issues. That he should really talk to Lea about himself."

"Lea doesn't have issues, but she has her own litany of insecurities and hang-ups and reservations like every other person on the planet," Maribel says. "Also she claims she's done with him. Because she feels like she's always trying and he doesn't give her much to work with. Especially not lately."

"I guess there's not a ton we can do," Bailey says.

"Except smush their faces together and force them to kiss," Bianca says.

I shake my head at her seriously and Maribel does the same.

"Sounds like a good idea to me," Bailey says, oblivious to Maribel's and my dissent.

"Here's the thing though," Maribel says. "Lea expressly asked us not to talk to you guys about this."

"All right, we'll keep it on the down-low. We won't even tell Sam." Bailey is obviously not listening, so I tap him on the arm. "We won't mention this conversation to Sam, right?"

"Huh? Nah. Sam's staying at home all week anyway."

Maribel nods. "I think the plan should be that we just encourage them in the right direction. Prod them along," she says.

"Keep them on course," I say.

Bailey and Bianca are making faces at each other in the rearview mirror and I get the feeling we've completely lost them on this one.

"I'm going to take Bianca's duck face as agreement," I say.

Maribel shrugs. "I always do."

Sam (Gabe's brother)

On our way back to school after spring break Gabe seems relaxed, happy even.

"You're in a good mood," I say.

"I am. I'm really relieved about the hearing aid stuff, even if nothing's actually happening yet."

"So, how does it work?"

He shrugs. "First I have to decide exactly what kind is right for me. And then I have to go for a fitting."

"What's the plan with Lea?" I ask. "Now that you're taking care of your crap, it seems like maybe it's time to formulate a plan."

"There's no plan."

"Seriously?"

"For now I just want to concentrate on this hearing stuff," he says, not looking at me, pretending to be nonchalant as he hums along with the radio. "There's no way she likes me anyway."

"Or she thinks you don't like her because you refuse to speak in front of her."

"Or she has a boyfriend and all of this is moot."

"Or you have shown absolutely zero interest in her every

time you're in her presence and therefore she cannot be held accountable for having gone out and found herself a boyfriend who is willing to engage her in conversation."

He turns around and looks at my feet. "I don't know what to say, so what's the point?"

"The point is . . . you like her," I say. "The point is you talk about her all the time, and you want to be around her. So, figure out your crap and talk to her."

"Yeah, because it's that easy."

"All right, what about . . . if you practice talking to some other girl. Some girl you don't really like, but who you see around?"

"I don't know. Why would I bother?"

"For practice, dumbass. Do you even listen to me?"

He gives me a meaningful look.

"Fine. I know, sometimes you don't hear, blah, blah, blah. But I'm serious, Gabe, try talking to some other girl. Maybe gain a little confidence."

"I don't have a lot of options," he says, his face full of thought like he's moving through a mental Rolodex of females willing to be in his presence.

"So next time we're at a party, just talk to someone."

"Yeah, that's not really . . ."

"Or what about that other girl in your creative writing class. The one who's sort of flaky and annoying?"

"Hillary?"

"Yeah. Try talking to her."

"Huh, you know, that might just work," he says, nodding. "Between this fairly decent advice and Casey's whole thing about desensitization, I think you morons are finally starting to earn your keep."

"Keep talking like that and I'm going to make you get out and walk."

"I'll tell Mom on you."

APRIL

Hillary (*creative writing classmate*)

Gabe and Lea haven't been talking much lately. Basically since spring break. They were all over each other at the beginning of the semester, but it's been at least two or three weeks since I've seen them giggling and inside-joking and quoting lame, dorky TV shows together. They don't even sit next to each other anymore. I bet they had a huge fight.

I know this is my chance to swoop in. Check my hair, check my makeup, put on extra lip gloss, and wait for Inga to stop talking and then make my move. I'll start simple. Don't want to scare him away. He's a little bit skittish.

"Hey, Gabe," I say, twirling a piece of hair.

"Hey," he says. He watches as Lea leaves without so much as a wave. Don't let the door hit you in the ass on the way out, I think, watching her go.

"What are you up to?"

"I dunno," he says, closing his notebook.

"I was going to go up to the student center to get something to eat." I like how he's looking at me, the way he's watching my lips move so attentively. It's got be the Berry Bloom Lip Shine. It's so seductive, not even Gabe can withstand its powers.

"Oh, okay. I was, um, going up there anyway," he says.

"Awesome." He is the cutest.

We walk up the stairs and I try to talk to him, but he doesn't respond. When we get outside, I ask what he's working on for his final project. But his answer is boring, so I try a new topic.

"What did you do for spring break?"

"Nothing. I worked, went down to Atlantic City one night with my brother and our friends."

"Sounds terrible," I say.

"It was actually kind of fun," he says.

"Oh, well, that's cool. I went to Negril. You should totally go to Jamaica sometime."

"It's not really my speed," he says.

I let the topic drop because it's kind of boring to talk about with someone who doesn't get it. "Are you graduating next year?" I ask.

We're about to walk into the student center now and he's still totally engrossed with my lips. I wish I could take a second to put on more lip gloss. I feel like it's fading since I'm talking so much. I'll have to slip into the bathroom or something.

"Uh. No. I'm technically still a sophomore, credit-wise. I missed most of my sophomore year because . . ." I zone out. He's not a particularly captivating storyteller. I zone back in around the time he says something about losing a baseball scholarship.

But he doesn't even offer to pay for my salad. That's disappointing. He's cute though, so I'll let it slide for now.

Maribel (Lea's roommate)

"Lea," I hiss into my phone.

"Maribel?"

"Gabe is at this very moment eating lunch in the student center with Hillary the skank queen of Cockblock-ville!"

"NO!"

"YES!"

"Shit."

"Exactly."

"Why is he doing that? There's no way he likes her. She's so vapid."

"Vapid is such a great word."

"Isn't it?"

"Totally."

"Okay, what's happening between them?"

"Um, hold on, let me see if I can get a little bit closer without being noticed."

"Be cool, Mar. We don't need him seeing you."

I stealthily move through the student center food court area, peering between tables and around corners, trying my best not to arouse suspicions. When I find a good vantage point, I'm a little surprised to find that I'm out of breath. I need to start working out.

"All right, I'm kind of around the corner and now I can peek over there and it looks like she's talking and he's not saying anything."

"Yeah, that sounds like Gabe," she says, the affection apparent in her voice.

"He just touched her hand!"

"What? No!" Lea exclaims. "Not possible. I don't believe it."

"He totally did."

"This is terrible, Mar," she says. "Now what's happening?"

"She's laughing and he's smiling. They're both eating, I think. Oh my God, she's touching his foot with her foot."

"Are you sure you're looking at the right couple?"

"Yes, I'm not an idiot."

"Why do I feel like this? I thought I was trying to get over him."

"I don't know," I tell her honestly.

"This is terrible, Maribel. I totally messed up. I can't believe that I basically let him slip through my fingers."

I sigh heavily on Lea's behalf.

"Maybe he doesn't like me. That must be it. I'm sure I've been reading all the signals wrong. The only reason he talks to me is so that he can copy my homework or something."

"How would he even go about copying your homework for creative writing?"

"I don't know. My emotions are spiraling out of control. I never promised I would be logical at a time like this!"

"Maybe I should go up to them and interrupt and he see how he reacts?"

"Yes, and keep me on the phone so I can listen in."

"This is the true meaning of friendship," I tell her.

"Thank you, Maribel. Your kindness and spying will be remembered for many years to come."

I hold my phone in my hand, making sure the speaker will face them when I get to the table, without it looking like I'm obviously trying to get the speaker to face them.

"Hey, Gabe," I say as I get close.

"Hey, Maribel," he says.

"How's it going?"

"Oh, pretty okay," he says, smiling up at me, innocent as can be. "Do you know Hillary?"

I look over at her and she smiles the fakest smile the world has ever known.

"What are you guys up to?"

"I asked Gabe out for lunch after class today and he said yes," she says, touching his hand, AGAIN.

For his part, Gabe looks less than thrilled.

"Yeah. I was coming here anyway," he says.

"I think we should definitely do this again sometime though," Hillary says.

I'm starting to feel super weird and Gabe is starting to look a little bit scared.

"You know, I'm done here," he says, standing abruptly. "Where are you headed, Maribel?"

"Um," I say, raising my eyebrows, trying to decide whether or not to help Gabe out of this situation, but also knowing that I need to get rid of Lea somehow. I hit "end" on my phone and pray that she understands. "I was heading home."

He smiles at me and collects his belongings.

"Cool, I'll walk out with you. See you," he says to Hillary.

"Um," is all she squeaks out, shaking her head in disbelief.

"Sorry about that," he says to me as we leave the student center. "I couldn't hang out with her for even like ten more seconds."

"It's fine, I don't mind being used."

He smiles. "Is Lea with you?"

"She's at home."

He nods. "Well, I'm off to work, but thanks for helping me out of that one."

"Yeah, no problem," I say. "Anytime."

I watch him walk away and find that I have four missed calls from Lea. It's a good thing I had my phone on silent or that could have been highly suspicious. I call her back.

"How did you have time to call me four times in the past three minutes?"

"What is going on? I can't handle this!"

"It's all good, babycakes," I tell her. "He used my presence to get away from the skank queen. And now he's gone to work."

"I still don't like it," she says.

"I swear to you, it's okay."

"Okay, cool, thanks."

"He asked about you again," I tell her.

"Interesting," she says.

"It is, right?"

"Interesting how he's always asking about me behind my back and then not talking to me in front of my face. And then going out on dates with Hillary."

"This doesn't really seem like you, to get this angry."

She sighs. "I know, I know. I'm upset about being upset. I'm tired of going around in circles like this. And I'm so embarrassed."

"Embarrassed about what? You haven't done anything to be embarrassed about. You like a boy, it happens," I say.

"I think I just need to focus on getting over him. I'm not built for this emotional roller coaster."

"I get it. I'll do whatever I can to help. We'll do some type of program. Getting over Gabe in twelve easy steps."

"Thanks, Maribel. You're awesome."

"I know. I'll be home soon."

"I'll start working on the rehab program."

Charlotte (a barista)

"Lea's here," I whisper to Keith as she wanders in.

"Oh, yay!" he says. "I haven't seen her in so long."

She goes through the line quickly, ordering an iced mocha and then taking her usual seat in the corner near the window. And within minutes, Gabe appears. He has great timing.

"It's like he stalks her," I mutter to Keith.

"Seriously. His timing is uncanny."

Gabe steps through the door, obviously looking around for Lea. He sees her, but she doesn't immediately see him. She's got earbuds in, so it stands to reason that she's totally zoned out.

Gabe comes through the line, ordering his usual grande coffee, room for milk.

"Pike Place," he adds with a smile before I can even offer the options.

"You seem chipper today," I say. I don't mean to say it, I really don't. I just can't help myself anymore.

He smiles shyly. "Things are looking up," he says with a shrug.

They're nice people, albeit misguided and obviously having issues getting a normal relationship off the ground. But compared to a lot of other people who frequent this establishment, they're courteous and sweet.

So much better than the people who take their coffee orders far too personally, who have deep-seated emotional issues about how many pumps of mocha they get.

Not to mention how nice Gabe was to me when I told him about my broken foot. And his confession about his car accident made me like him even more. Because he didn't have to share; he *wanted* to.

I hand him his coffee and he goes over to put milk and sugar in. The whole time he's watching Lea. He swallows heavily a bunch of times in a row and then he touches his ear. I guess he can feel me looking at him because he turns around and smiles at me. I give him a thumbs-up.

"Keith," I say. "I think something's about to happen."

Keith looks up from where he's preparing a chai latte and into the corner. I have the distinct urge to turn the elevator music down, but I have to keep helping customers. I almost tell this one old lady to shut her trap so I can hear what's happening.

He walks over to Lea's table and she doesn't notice him because she's still got her earbuds in. He touches her shoulder and she looks up.

"Miss?" the guy at the front of the line says. I shush him. I just need two seconds to hear what's going to happen over there. Keith stops steaming milk and I swear even the Starbucks sound system holds its breath.

I think he says hi to her, and she says hi back. He gestures toward the chair opposite her and she makes what I read as a hand motion of surrender rather than of welcoming. That doesn't bode well.

"It's all yours," I hear her say. Her voice is loud, tinged with too much emotion for such a benign request from Gabe. Then she closes up her books, shoves them in her bag, and leaves. Gabe is obviously stunned.

I look over at Keith, who looks almost as sad as I feel.

"All right, what do you want?" I ask the old man.

"Some service!" he says indignantly.

I give the man his coffee and then signal to Keith that I'm going over to talk to Gabe. There's no one in line at the moment and hopefully it'll stay that way while I'm gone. I honestly can't believe I'm getting involved in this, but he looks so sad, I feel like I have to at least ask him if he's okay.

I approach his table, grabbing for a rag so I can pretend to be wiping down the tables around it. "You okay?" I ask when he sees me looking at him.

"I don't know what I did wrong."

"Maybe you waited too long?"

He chews his fingernail and nods at me.

"I'm sorry," I say sincerely.

"Thank you. I'm going to sit here and pick up the pieces of my crushed ego."

"Would a piece of free cheesecake help?"

"Free cheesecake could probably help almost anything."

"I'll be back in a jiffy."

I hate myself for getting involved. And for saying the word "jiffy."

Sam *(Gabe's brother)*

Gabe and Bailey show up several hours before the party will even start.

"Food, liquor run," Gabe says by way of greeting.

"Lovely to see you, too," I say back.

"Gabe's in a pissy mood," Bailey tells me. "Don't mind him."

"What's up?" I ask, turning toward him.

"I'm not pissy, I'm confused and kind of sad," he says to Bailey, but completely ignores my question.

"What's up with Gabe?" I ask Bailey.

"Come on," he says. "I'll tell you about it while we go find food and booze."

"Lemme go find Casey. I think he's driving."

The four of us pile into my car, Gabe pouting in the back-seat, while we go through the McDonald's drive-through. Bailey fills us in on everything that's been going on. Casey parks and I start handing out food.

"So, Gabe-o decided that he should be the one to tell Lea about the party tonight. But he balked every time he saw her this week and totally chickened out."

"I wasn't chickening out," he grumbles. "I didn't want to mention it in class in front of Hillary, and well, fine, the other time I saw her I chickened out. But she was with that guy again!"

"Fine. He chickened out once. Then he saw her at Starbucks yesterday and worked up his nerve and did a little dance and all the baristas were cheering him on—"

"You're totally telling this story wrong," Gabe says.

"Fine," Bailey says. "You tell it."

Gabe takes a huge bite of his Big Mac and then slides forward. "There are these baristas and I see them all the time, and they're usually pretty nice, except for the one who can be kind of bitchy sometimes, but even she was being nice yesterday. She said I was chipper. And I was chipper. It was warm out and I got an A on my paper for Foreign Policy and I went to Starbucks hoping to see Lea and she was mag-ically there."

"Okay," I say. Casey nods along.

"I walked up to her and she had her earbuds in so I tapped

her on the shoulder. She looked up at me and pulled them out. And I said hi, and she said hi."

"So far this sounds okay."

"Yeah, and then I asked if I could sit down at her table and she said it was 'all mine' and then she got up and left."

"Just like that?"

"Just like that," he responds.

"That doesn't sound like Lea."

"I know. But the sometimes-bitchy barista, Charlotte, felt so bad for me that she gave me a free piece of cheesecake."

"Score."

"Silver lining," he says with a shrug.

"What are you gonna do?" I ask.

"I don't know," he says.

"You do seem awfully chipper for someone who basically got rejected by the girl he likes yesterday. I mean, aside from the obvious grumbliness earlier."

"Oh, well. I got my hearing aid." He turns to show me his ear.

"Oh, yeah, Mom told me," I say.

Then Gabe turns to show the other guys.

"Basically invisible," Bailey says.

"I don't see anything," Casey says, squinting.

Gabe takes the tiny piece of plastic out of his ear and we ooh and ahh over it.

"They mailed it to me after the fitting last week. It just

came in today." He slips it back into his ear. "I still kind of hate talking about it, but being able to hear has really improved my mood."

"Yeah, that's not exactly a shocker," I say.

"Hey, man, if I want to sit around and wallow for a year and a half about my hearing that's my prerogative," he says, but he's smiling.

We head into the liquor store, still trying to come up with a solution for Gabe.

"At least you'll be able to hear tonight," I say, coming up next to him in the vodka aisle.

"I think it'll help."

Bailey approaches Gabe and me. "I could talk to Bianca and have her talk to Lea," Bailey says.

"I know, and I appreciate that, but I feel like I should take care of this myself."

Bailey nods. "Let me know if you change your mind."

We head back to my house after that, hanging out in our room.

By the time the party starts we're all pretty seriously drunk. And by the time Lea and her friends show up, the room is spinning for me. The girls head downstairs to the basement and we follow behind them. Bailey and Bianca disappear almost immediately, finding some hidden corner.

"Looking at her makes me feel all . . . rage-y," Gabe says to me and Casey, staring across the room at Lea. "I want to yell."

"You're not a big yeller," Casey notes.

"Settle down, big boy. You don't need to yell at her," I say.

He takes a swig of his beer. "Why have we been playing this stupid shitty game for an entire year?"

"Center your chi, harness your rage," Casey says. "Are you actually being drunk and belligerent? That's not like you."

"I just want to understand." He continues to stare at her. She finally looks over and raises her eyebrows at him. And it's like Gabe's signal to let all of his thoughts out.

Maribel (Lea's roommate)

"Hey, Lea," a voice says behind me. Lea's jaw drops, so I turn around and I'm not particularly shocked to see Gabe there. This was all bound to come to a head sooner or later. I figured it might be tonight. I kind of hoped it would be tonight.

"Where's your boyfriend tonight?" he asks.

"I don't have a boyfriend," she says, making a slightly disgusted face.

We did some fairly serious pregaming before coming. And it took a lot of coercion to even get Lea here. She said she was done with Gabe and tired of playing games with him. But Bianca really wanted to come hang out with Bailey. Then we got Lea drunk and she decided that she needed to see Gabe, just to prove to herself that she's over him.

Looking at her face right now makes me confident that she is definitely not over him.

"Oh yeah? Who's that dude I keep seeing you around campus with? The tall, skinny dude with the glasses," Gabe asks. He's quite obviously drunk, but the thing about Gabe is that he's not a threatening drunk. He's like a tall, lanky puppy who doesn't have control over his limbs.

"My friend Danny?" Lea asks, still looking confused. Then she goes into full-on Lea anger and pokes her finger into his chest, making him back up against the wall. "You're one to talk!"

Gabe's eyes go wide.

"You and your footsie lunch date with Hillary the skank queen of Cockblock-ville."

He looks terrified. I feel like I should protect him, but I'm pretty sure I'm supposed to be on Lea's side in all of this. I notice Casey and Sam come to stand next to me.

"Hey," I say out of the corner of my mouth. "Should we be worried about this?"

"I think they're going to work it out for themselves," Casey says.

"Yeah, Gabe seemed pretty resolute," Sam adds.

"Finally," I say.

Gabe looks at us. "I can hear the three of you, you know."

"Oh, now you can hear everything!" Lea says.

"I can. I got a hearing aid," he tells her, tipping his chin up imperiously.

"Bully for you!" Lea says, throwing her hands in the air. "You know, you could have told me a hundred years ago about stuff and then I wouldn't have been wondering all of these hundreds of years about stuff and maybe we could have been doing stuff."

"That was a lot of 'stuff's," Casey whispers.

"I can hear you, too," Lea says, whipping around and staring daggers at Casey.

He holds up his hands in surrender.

"You know," Gabe says, "I was trying to be nice to you yesterday. I was going to ask you to come to this party and you totally ignored me."

"I didn't want to talk to you," she says, her voice metered.

"But why not? What did I do?"

"I don't know, you ask my friends about me all the time but never talk to me? We see each other places and you barely even say hi? But then sometimes you magically, out of nowhere, want to be friends with me? But only when it's convenient to you."

He looks at her and blinks.

"Any of that ringing a bell?"

"It's not only when it's convenient for me. . . ."

"It's a lot of mixed signals, Gabe. You're cute and nice and quirky and good weird one minute, and then not very nice and kind of standoffish and bad weird the next minute."

"I don't mean to ever be bad weird," he says quietly. "I mean, I always want to be nice and cute. I never want to be the other stuff. I'm not trying to be that stuff. But maybe I really am all that stuff, because I didn't even know I was doing that."

"A lot of 'stuffs' again," Sam says. "Maybe we should make a drinking game out of it."

I take a small step back. "I feel like we shouldn't be listening to this," I tell him.

"Shh," Casey says, pulling me back closer. "They'll need our recollection of this blessed event because they're both so drunk."

"I'm not that drunk," Lea says without turning around.

"I am," Gabe says. "For the record."

"So what do you have to say for yourself?" Lea says, stabbing him in the chest again with her finger.

"Please stop stabbing me in the chest," he says.

She puts her arms at her sides and balls her hands in fists. "Fair enough."

He looks at her, his face some expression that I don't quite know how to read, and for a second I think he might lean down and kiss her. I worry about that, because I'm pretty sure she'd knee him in the junk if he did that right now.

"All that stuff is right and if I was normal and not bad weird, I would have told you stuff and we could have been doing stuff," he says.

"I like how vague this is," Casey mumbles. "Their overuse of the word 'stuff' is epic."

"Seriously, I've started drinking every time they use the word 'stuff,'" Sam says.

"What's going on?" Bianca asks, coming up beside me.

"I think Gabe and Lea are either about to get into an epic fistfight or possibly start making out," I explain, glancing over at her and Bailey.

"Make out, make out, make out," Bailey starts chanting quietly.

Gabe doesn't even look over, just points at him and says, "Shut up."

Bailey shuts up.

"Well," Lea says. "Is that it? Is that really all you have to say for yourself?"

Gabe looks at her, and then at each of us in turn, frowning. He looks back at Lea. "I don't think I can do this here, in front of all these people. Can we at least go outside or something? Would that be okay?"

I wait for her to start yelling again, but it's like all the fight has gone out of her.

"Yeah, of course, that's fine," she says, crossing her arms.

I feel like I should say something, but I don't want to accidentally talk her out of it. They really do need to talk.

"You sure, Lea?" Bianca says, reading my mind.

"Yeah. I'm cool. I'll shoot you guys a text if I need you."

We all just look at each other. And then we look behind us and find that the party as a whole had basically come to a stop to watch what was happening. Lea and Gabe make their way toward the stairs without another word.

The music gets louder again and everyone starts talking. Casey goes to get us all a beer from his secret stash.

"And now we wait," he says, handing us each a bottle.

I turn to Casey once they're out of sight up the stairs and ask, "I don't want to wait. Is there somewhere we can spy on them?"

"Do you really want to do that?" he asks, making a face.

"Dude," Bailey says. "There's no way that you don't want to do that. Don't act noble now, we just need to find the prime location for eavesdropping on them."

We go up the stairs and into the living room, cracking open the front window, but they seem to be standing closer to the other side of the house.

"Maybe we need to go in the bathroom," Casey says, and the rest of us follow him in. Bailey locks the door behind us.

"We don't need to get interrupted during such an important surveillance operation," he explains.

Casey cracks open the window and a gust of fresh air comes into the bathroom. We keep the light off and we all breathe as quietly as possible.

"You should have a coat," we hear Gabe say.

"Such a Gabe thing to say," Sam notes.

"I don't need a coat," Lea says. "What did you want to talk about?"

"I don't know. I just couldn't think in there anymore. It was like the whole party was staring at us and listening to us. And there was just too much I wanted to say for it to be on display like that."

Lea crosses her arms. "So say it."

"I guess, for starters, I'm sorry. I'm really bad at this stuff."

"What stuff? We're both overusing the word 'stuff' tonight, like we're so afraid to say anything specific we're saying nothing at all."

"Bailey, tell whoever is banging on the door to stop, we need to continue eavesdropping," I whisper.

Bailey cracks open the bathroom door.

"I'm going to piss in the kitchen sink if you don't let me in there," Antonio says.

"Antonio has to piss," Bailey tells us. We file out of the bathroom and run around the house trying to find a vantage point as good as the one we had. We end up in an upstairs bedroom but their voices mostly get carried away on the breeze. We can hear Lea yell sometimes, but that's about it.

"Guess we're going to have to wait for their recap in the morning," I say.

––––––––––––

Victor *(creative writing classmate)*

I have been avoiding Gabe and Lea like my life depends on it. For the past three months or so, every time I've seen one of them, I literally run in the opposite direction. Because where one is, usually the other is close behind. And I am so freaking tired of getting caught up in their little "moments."

On my way to this house party tonight with my roommates I didn't even think of Gabe and Lea. That's my own fault. Because of course they're here. And of course they started some kind of weird scene in the basement. As soon as I realized who was causing such a ruckus, I saw myself out and decided to hang in the side yard and chain-smoke.

And wouldn't you know, I'm about two drags into my first cigarette when I hear them out in front of the house. I can't catch a break. I consider stubbing out the cigarette, but I don't want to waste it, so I stare at the sky and try to ignore them.

I pretend their voices are gentle waves lapping upon the shore. I focus on the stars and the way the wispy clouds move across the moon. And it starts making me very dizzy. Holy crap, I'm drunk.

I hear the murmur of Gabe's voice but not the words.

I decide I'm too curious not to watch the proceedings, so I stand up and move down the side of the house, trying to stay in the shadows, until I can see them through the bushes. I'm not sure how I got here—basically stalking the two people I claim to hate most in the world. I blame the booze.

Lea has her hands on her hips and Gabe is standing a million feet away from her. His hands are stuffed deep into his pockets and he's half turned in the opposite direction, like he's ready to run at the drop of a hat.

"Come on, Gabe, at least give me something to work with."

"I didn't want to date Hillary."

"So you wanted to be friends with her?"

"No."

"Good, 'cause she sucks."

"It's lame, you're going to think I'm so lame, I don't even think I can say it." He stares at the sky rather than looking at her.

"What?"

"I was using Hillary to practice."

"Practice what?" she asks, taking a step toward him.

He rolls his eyes. "I was using her to practice talking to girls."

I have to hold back a laugh. Lea doesn't say anything.

"I thought you understood that I was shy or whatever. That's why I picked that essay to read in class. I figured maybe you would be willing to be a little more patient with me because you understood. . . ."

"I did understand that. I still do, I accept that about you," she says. "But that was six months ago!"

"I'm slow."

"That's really, really slow, Gabe."

"I get nervous and then overthink things."

"You don't seem nervous right now."

"That's because I'm drunk right now!" he says.

"So, you're shy, and you're bad at talking to girls, and that's why you went out for lunch with Hillary?"

"It was just lunch at the student center. We weren't getting engaged. Why are you so stuck on this?"

"Because you were like . . . touching her hand and playing footsies."

"I touched her hand?"

"Yeah, Maribel was watching you the whole time and I was on the phone with her and she was giving me the play-by-play."

Oh, snap! There's no way he's getting himself out of this mess.

"You don't think that's maybe a little crazy?" he asks. "Having your friend watch me like that?"

"Well, maybe, but still. If you like me you wouldn't be doing that."

"Lea, the Hillary thing had nothing to do with you, not really. And you haven't exactly been forthright about your feelings. It's like I need a decoder ring to understand you. One day you're sitting with me in the diner and a few days later I see you flirting with some guy at the library, turning away from me, ignoring me."

She shakes her head. "I just got tired. And embarrassed. It was self-preservation."

"Yeah, I know that feeling," he says. He must catch sight of my cigarette then. "Who's over there?"

Lea turns around.

I step out from the side of the house. I try to smile, even though by the looks on their faces I'm about to get my ass whipped.

"Hey! How are you guys?"

"Victor," Lea says.

"Long time no see," I say, feigning friendliness.

"What are you doing here?" Gabe asks.

"I was at the party with my friends."

"Are you spying on us?" Lea asks.

"Yeah, just like you spied on Gabe," I say with a chuckle.

She scratches her nose nonchalantly. "Wow. That was quite the burn."

Gabe scoffs and turns away from me. "I'm gonna go."

"What? You're just gonna leave?" Lea asks.

"Yeah, I drank way too much to talk about this right now. And I feel like anything I say is going to come out wrong. And I want to figure this out. But I need to sleep first. It's not working right now."

"Because you're not listening to me."

"I don't think either of you are listening," I interject.

They both stare at me for a long minute. Then Gabe turns and gives Lea a look of surrender. "I'm sorry," he says.

We both watch him walk away.

"Maybe you should go after him," I say.

"Like I'm going to take advice from you," she snarls. She pushes past me and heads back inside, the door slamming behind her.

That didn't go well for any of us.

Two seconds later, she's slamming back out the door and calling over her shoulder, "No, really, I'm fine. I swear."

Her friends file out behind her. "You can't go alone."

"I'm not," Lea says. "Victor's going with me."

"Victor from creative writing?"

"Yes."

"You hate him."

Then a couple of guys fall out of the door. "Where's Gabe?"

"He left," she says simply.

"Where did he go?"

She shrugs and pulls me along behind her, leaving a herd of confused drunk kids in her wake. I wave at them.

I suppose I could use a walk.

Bob (a bus driver)

I'm taking a break outside the student center and my old friend Gabe stumbles onto the bus. He nods his head at me and I can't help but notice he looks distraught. I glance at him in the rearview and he looks kinda sick to his stomach.

"You gonna ralph?" I ask him, catching his eye in the mirror.

"Nope. Just a crappy night."

"You wanna talk about it?"

He opens his mouth, but then we hear a girl's voice right outside the bus.

"Perfect," Gabe mutters.

"Okay, so thanks for walking me," she says. I realize pretty quick that it's Lea and that she's maybe the source of Gabe's crappy night.

"What?" the kid outside asks.

"Thanks for walking with me. I needed to get away from my friends and you did me a solid. But I need to be alone right now. I don't want to hang out or anything."

"Where are we?" the kid asks.

"Student center. Just head a block that way and you'll get back to the party."

"You okay out there?" I call through the door.

"Yup," she says, turning and smiling sweetly at me. "We're good."

"I should go?" he asks.

"Yes, and don't you dare ever tell anyone what I said to you on the way here."

"I don't . . . even," the guy mumbles. "You said . . . stuff?"

"Good, keep it that way."

He heads back in the other direction and Lea steps onto the bus.

"You sure he's okay?" I ask.

She makes a guilty face and then shakes her head. "Yeah, he's okay. His friends are still there and it's not that far of a walk."

She takes a deep breath and lets it out in a long slow sigh when she sees Gabe.

"Of course," she murmurs.

"I'm on break for another ten," I tell them.

They both nod. She takes a seat behind him.

They sit in stony silence for a few moments and then he turns in his seat.

"I'm sorry I was being so belligerent," he says.

"I'm sorry I was so cold to you yesterday at Starbucks," she says.

I start up the bus and I drive the route I'm supposed to. I don't think either of them noticed they got on going in the wrong direction, so it's going to take extra time to get them to their side of campus.

"I know I said I didn't want to talk right now, but there

are things you should know."

She nods and looks less tense.

"So, here's the deal," he says.

I glance at them in the rearview mirror while we're sitting at a stoplight. She's leaning on his seat and he's still sitting sideways, but he's not looking at her anymore, instead he's focused on his lap. There's something about the way she has her hands folded under her chin that makes me think she wants to touch him but she's holding back.

"First of all, this is really embarrassing, but I've never had a girlfriend or anything and I was worried that I would do something wrong."

Lea shrugs. "I've only had one long-term boyfriend. It's not exactly like I'm Elizabeth Taylor going on her fortieth husband or something."

"Really?"

"Really."

"That does make me feel better."

"See? Look at how easy it is," she says, smiling.

"This one is harder, because it's not that big of a deal anymore, but it's important for you to know, because I think you'll understand me a little better."

She nods patiently.

"January of last year I was in a car accident," he starts. "Right after New Year's."

She gasps a tiny breath. I'm not even sure how I hear over the noise of the bus engine.

"I was driving back from dropping my little sister Becca off at a sleepover and I hit some ice and my car spun around and slammed into a tree, right in the driver's side. I broke my elbow and I hit my head really hard on the door." He touches his ear and the side of his head unconsciously.

He glances at her and I realize that I sat through this light twice already. Good thing there's no one else around right now. I start driving again, but my focus is with the kids. I always say we shouldn't be out on the roads when it's icy.

"I'm sorry," she says quietly.

"It's okay! That's the thing. I'm okay. I was unconscious for a couple of days and there were a couple of weeks where I was in the hospital and everything hurt. And I needed help with pretty much everything and my mom bought me a lot of shoes without laces since I was in casts for so long and couldn't tie my shoes." He smiles at her then, but she looks too stricken to smile back.

"Okay."

"But it turns out that when I hit my head, I basically . . . broke something in my ear. And that's why I can't hear out of it. There's more to it than that, boring medical stuff, but that's the gist. And the doctor said it might get better or it might not. I kept waiting for it to get better. And my elbow got better, and my head. But not my ear."

She nods.

"And then I came back to school after being gone so long and I lost my baseball scholarship. Everything just sucked so much all the time," he says. This kid is killing me. "I wanted you to like me, but I didn't want you to feel sorry for me. I didn't want anyone to feel sorry for me. So instead I messed everything up."

We're at their stop now and I don't know whether to tell them or not. Lea notices and stands.

"Thank you," she says to him. "For telling me."

"So we're good?"

"Yeah. I just . . ." She pauses and sighs. "I feel like things have been weird and crazy and if maybe you had told me this sooner, I would have understood. But I had almost nothing to work with."

He nods, but he looks like he's bracing himself for a punch in the face.

"Can I have some time? To think?" Lea asks.

"Okay."

"I'm sorry. It's a lot to take in." She crosses her arms and it's like she finally remembers that I'm there. She holds up a finger, asking me to wait one minute.

"Oh."

"It's not a bad thing. But I lied before about how drunk I was, and you're drunk, and I don't know that we can resolve all these months of stupidity in one night."

He digs the heels of his hands into his eyes.

"Walk me home?" she asks. "Please?"

He nods and they walk down the aisle, both of them thanking me, always on their best behavior even when they're obviously having an emotional night.

I watch them walk until they disappear into their building.

Casey (Gabe's friend)

I'm sitting on the porch pretending to read for my abnormal psych class. It's a gorgeous Sunday afternoon. The sun is out, the birds are shitting all over my car, and the chair I'm sitting on is groaning underneath me every time I shift around. I probably shouldn't have it tipped back with my feet propped up on the railing, but there's something about living dangerously that gets any civil engineer's heart racing. I'm testing the tensile strength. At least that's what I'll say when I get to the emergency room after it collapses out from under me.

"Why are you reading *I Never Promised You a Rose Garden*?"

I didn't even notice Gabe approach the house. The chair almost gives out as I flail around to right it. It does make a horrible squealing sound as the two front legs hit the floor.

"Abnormal psych," I say, while he laughs at my near fall. "Stop laughing at me."

He snorts, and then makes a serious face as he takes the other chair.

"So, what's up?" I ask. I have at least four hundred other questions I would like to ask, but I figure I should start with a fairly innocuous one.

"Nothing."

"Something's up."

"Well, yeah. But I don't know how to talk about it."

"We could play twenty questions. Starting with where did you go last night?"

"I went home."

"Why didn't you text one of us so we didn't think you were dead?"

He gives me an exasperated look.

"Fine, we knew you weren't dead. But you should have come back inside."

"No way, it was too humiliating. I couldn't deal."

"She left, too."

"Yeah, I know. We ran into each other on the bus."

"Yeah?"

"And I pretty much bared my soul to her and she was like, 'Cool, let's pick this up some other time.'"

"Seriously?"

"I guess I was giving too many mixed signals and like . . . not giving her enough to work with. And she said we were both too drunk to come to any decent conclusions last night.

And as we were walking into our building, she said she'd let me know when she was ready to talk."

"What are you going to do?"

"Do?"

"Yeah, what's the next step?"

"I'm not sure yet."

"I'm proud of you for acknowledging that there should be a next step."

"Yes, there should be, but I feel like I need to take a cue from her. Like I'll get a sign that she's ready to continue the conversation or whatever."

"You should go for some kind of romantic gesture."

"Oh, yeah, that sounds like me."

"So, make it a Gabe-esque romantic gesture."

"I can't even imagine what that might entail."

"Wait, before we get completely off track, was there a reason you came here?"

"Yeah, I was looking for some mindless entertainment in the form of video games."

"I think we can manage that."

MAY

Hillary (creative writing classmate)

"Sorry I ran a little late. Allergies," Inga says, rushing into the classroom at the last second. She looks like Rudolph the Red-Nosed Reindeer.

I really can't wait for this semester to be over. Particularly now that I know that Gabe thinks he's too good for me. I'm tired of having to spend several hours a week in his presence.

"I'm making a last-minute change to the assignment that's due on Thursday." Inga's nasally voice pulls me out of my daydream.

A groan erupts from the class.

"It's going to be shorter than it used to be," she promises.

I look at her suspiciously. I have a feeling this is some kind of trick. Nothing is ever short and easy in this class.

"You're going to write a one-hundred-word description of someone without using any adjectives."

"What?" I ask. I must have heard wrong.

"One hundred words, no adjectives, describing someone."

"But adjectives are descriptive words." I'm trying to understand why Inga thinks this is something normal people can accomplish. Like you have to be some kind of writing genius to do well on this assignment.

"Yes, thank you, Hillary, I know what adjectives are."

"It's impossible," I say. I have to work hard not to mumble "bitch" under my breath. Maybe her allergy medicine is making her stupid.

That must be it, because she literally rolls her eyes. Teachers aren't supposed to roll their eyes. I should report her for being a bitch. I look over at Gabe doodling in a notebook and then over to Lea, who's chewing her thumbnail. A glance around the rest of the room shows that all of the other students are also blasé about this ridiculous assignment. I slide down in my chair and cross my arms.

"Okay. Here's an example: 'My mom has a chair in her living room and when she sits in that chair the way she holds herself is relaxed. When she reads a book in that chair, it's like her habitat. When she settles down for an evening in that chair all is right in her world.' Can you picture my mom? The kind of person my mom is?"

"I guess . . ." I say, making sure to keep my attitude at maximum strength. If Inga can be bitchy then so can I.

"You could also say that someone has the face of a weasel, and their hair is straw, and their demeanor reminds you of a poodle that thinks too much of itself."

Oh, you better not be talking about me. I'm about to leap out of my seat and show Inga who's boss when a quiet voice says, "Sounds kinda cool."

Gabe's cute expression helps tamp down my anger. Until I remember that he's a complete dorkface and I can't stand him. Why is my life so complicated?

"Good," Inga says. "And everyone is going to have to read theirs in class. It's going to be twenty percent of your final. The other eighty percent will still be your series of story prompts as previously discussed."

Gabe audibly gulps. What did I ever see in him?

"I promise it'll be okay," Inga says, looking right at him. What the hell? Why is she such a weirdo perv?

I'm so glad this year is almost over.

Charlotte (a barista)

It's so busy I don't even notice her until she's right in front of me, picking up her beverage.

"Hey," I say.

"Oh, hey."

She seems bummed. I want to at least ask if she's okay but the line is out of control and the steam wand is making pterodactyl noises. It's not exactly a great moment for chitchat.

She takes her iced grande caramel macchiato and sits at the closest table, staring out the window. I have to wonder if she's trying to will Gabe into the store using only the powers of her mind. I watch her out of the corner of my eye until my hour on drink duty is up. She has a little pink notebook out and she's scribbling away.

Of course she has a little pink notebook.

I'm shocked it's not covered in faux fur or something.

I meander toward her under the guise of wiping down tables. She looks over at me, and smiles, tight-lipped, and it doesn't reach her eyes.

One of her friends literally sashays through the door then.

"Lea my love," he says, and she looks up from her notebook. "How are things?"

"Hey, Danny. Things have been better," she says.

"Tell me your troubles," he says.

I eavesdrop on them as I wipe down the tables better than they have ever been wiped down in the history of Starbucks. But when she gets to the part where she told Gabe she needed more time, I can't contain myself one more second.

"You did what?" I ask, stepping right up to the table.

"We were drunk," she says, looking up at me, shaking her head. "It was bad timing. Everything felt wrong."

"He's like pretty much in love with you, you know," I say.

"What?"

"He never stops looking at you, when you're here together. I've heard him ask people about you when you're not around. I've heard him talking about you."

"She's totally right," Danny says.

"I messed up," Lea says.

"Listen," I say, sighing and taking the seat across from her, hoping my manager doesn't notice. "I thought he was a complete asshole. Like a total flake and not really worth anyone's time. But over the past few months, he's changed my mind. We love watching you guys."

"We?"

"Um, basically everyone who works here, but in particular Tabitha and Keith."

That makes her smile for real this time.

"So, I guess I'm saying give it another shot. It can't hurt."

"I agree," Danny says.

"Okay," she says. "I think I have a plan."

Victor (creative writing classmate)

I hear Gabe before I see him. I mean, I have no idea when I hear the movement that it's going to be Gabe, because had I known it was Gabe I would have run quietly in the other direction. He's shelving books in the library and I need a book from the exact place he's working. There's no way around this confrontation.

When he sees me, I get the distinct feeling he's more afraid of me than I am of him.

"Hey, man," I say.

He grunts a response and barely glances at me.

"Did you and your girl work everything out the other night?"

He scoffs.

"I guess not."

"Why would you care?" he asks, his voice quiet and steady.

"I feel like a shit about it. I should have walked away. Instead I got involved and somehow I made things worse. And I'm sorry."

He rolls his eyes and moves down to the next section.

"I'm serious."

"Cool," he says, his voice sort of pinched now, uncomfortable.

"And I'm sorry about what I said on the last day of creative writing last semester. I guess I thought maybe you would use it as a push in the right direction. It's so obvious that she likes you, bro."

"Ha."

"No, I'm serious."

"Yeah, right. Why am I supposed to believe you?"

"Because for some reason I keep getting stuck inside your little . . . moments. I was there at midnight breakfast, and at that show in January, and the other night. Not to mention all those classes last semester."

He turns to look at me. Apparently now I have his attention.

"And you two assholes are the most annoyingly cute thing I've ever seen. I'm annoyed at myself for even using the word 'cute.' I feel sick to my stomach over using that word."

That makes him chuckle.

"I have no clue why I'm getting involved, and at this point you would have every right to punch me in the face, but I guess before you do that, you should know that I might hate you guys, but you obviously don't hate each other."

"Well, after you left the other night, she got on the bus and I was there. She asked me to give her some time. So I'm giving her some time."

"Maybe you shouldn't have walked away in the first place."

"Did she say anything? While you guys were walking?"

"I hope you realize how deep my self-loathing goes that I'm even involved with this, but after you left I walked with her to the bus. And she talked about you the whole time. It wasn't always nice stuff, because she was pissed off, but it was like she couldn't stop. She made me promise not to tell anyone what she said, and I don't remember the specifics, but

I feel pretty confident in telling you that she never told me not to tell you she said it. Just not to tell anyone *what* she said."

He narrows his eyes at me and I can see him mouthing the last words I said. "I think I'm keeping up with you here."

"Yeah, I don't want to get kneed in the balls over this. I wouldn't put it past her to do something like that."

He smiles for real this time. "I can't believe I'm saying this, but thanks, Victor."

"I would totally be lying if I said 'anytime.'" I leave then before this becomes any more like a scene in a Lifetime movie.

Pam (Inga's wife)

"Aw, sweetheart, you look awful," I say to Inga as I come in Tuesday night after work.

"Thanks," she says, sniffling and blowing her nose.

"Well, you do look awful. And you sound worse. And I like to think that honesty is a key aspect of our relationship. The cornerstone even."

"Please stop babbling and make me some soup," she says, her voice sadder than her face.

"Of course."

Once the soup has been made and she's ensconced on the couch with more blankets and pillows, I take a seat in the armchair across from her. The blankets basically act as a force field, so there's no use trying to sit next to her on the couch.

"Ugh. I thought this was allergies and it definitely isn't."

"You should probably cancel class tomorrow."

"No!"

"Okay . . ."

"I have to go. I gave the assignment."

"Which assignment is that?"

"The describe someone without adjectives assignment."

"Oh, the big one."

"It was time. I needed to give them one last opportunity." She pauses to blow her nose. " 'Opportunity' is a hard word to say when you have a cold."

"I know, baby," I say sympathetically, even though I don't have personal experience with that issue.

"Anyway. If this doesn't work, at least I know I tried everything."

"You have. You have gone above and beyond what any sane person would ever, or should ever, do for a pair of random students in their creative writing class."

"Stop trying to make me feel ashamed for believing in the power of love."

"I'm not trying to make you feel ashamed! I'm trying to make you realize that there's nothing else you can do."

"I could have run a contest in class." Her eyes glaze over as her imagination runs wild. "And made them work in pairs, and then the prize would have been dinner at a restaurant."

I look at her doubtfully. "Wasn't that basically the plot of an episode of *Glee*?"

"No. Maybe. I don't remember, I've taken too much cold medicine."

"I'll make you some tea. That should help with the memory loss."

"Thank you!" she calls from the couch.

When I go back in barely three minutes later, she's passed out, drooling on the couch.

Maribel (*Lea's roommate*)

"Maribel?" Lea's voice whispers from across the room.

I don't respond.

"Maribel," she says again, this time louder.

I squeeze my eyes tightly closed and barely even breathe.

"Maribel, maybe I should have written about my dad, or my grandma, or one of the Starbucks baristas."

I think I might pass out from lack of oxygen when she throws a pillow at me.

"I know you're awake."

"Fine," I say, tossing it back and rolling onto my side. "But why are we discussing this again? You know where I stand on it."

"What if it's terrible? What if he doesn't appreciate it? What if he's too mad to care? What if he's decided to give up on me? What if I puke before I even have time to read it?"

"Lea. You are a wonderful person. He would be lucky to have you. But no one is forcing you to write this essay about him. You don't have to do anything you don't want to do," I tell her.

She's about to speak, but I cut her off, because I know what she's going to say.

"You need to stop obsessing."

"If it was that easy, believe me, I would have."

"I want to believe you, but it's four a.m., and we've had this same conversation at least a dozen times in the past two days. Now go to sleep so you can look perfect and wonderful tomorrow when you read to Gabe."

"All right. G'night."

"G'night."

It's quiet for a few minutes.

"But what am I going to wear?" she wails into the darkness.

Sam (Gabe's brother)

Gabe is sitting on a bench looking confused and lost. This is not an unusual look for him. He's always sort of been that guy.

"Hey, why did you want to meet?" I ask.

"I need your advice."

"Of course you do," I say, sitting down on the bench. "You just need your big brother sometimes. I totally get it."

"Can you read this?" he asks, handing me a sheet of paper and totally ignoring my big-brother comment.

"Um, sure." I glance it over. It's super short.

He looks at me expectantly.

"This is about Lea?"

He nods.

"It's good."

"Just good?"

"Well, yeah, I mean, what's it for? Are you going to randomly hand it to her?"

"No, I'm going to read it, in class today."

"Wow," I say. And I mean it. I read the two paragraphs over again.

"Is that too embarrassing?"

"It could be, potentially, but if she likes you even a little bit, this will totally win her over." I shake my head and read it again. "I feel like you reading it is . . . kind of amazing, actually."

"I'm terrified."

"It's big. It's bold. I would be shocked if you weren't."

"If I die of embarrassment or terror, tell Mom I love her."

He stands up to leave.

"Good luck," I say, seriously.

"Thanks."

Inga (creative writing professor)

I feel about as nervous as Gabe looks, which gives me hope that he took the bait. I know he did as soon as I call the class to order and he raises his hand.

"Gabe?"

"Can I go first?"

"Sure! I appreciate your enthusiasm."

He smiles weakly and takes a deep breath. He walks to the front of the class and I take a desk at the side. He's gotten better at sharing this semester. He's not the same kid he was when he stood up there back in the fall.

"All right, so." He clears his throat and looks at me, though I'm not sure if the look is "help me" or "this is a bad idea." "This is exactly a hundred words."

"Great. Whenever you're ready," I say.

He squeezes his eyes shut for a second and chews his lip, before opening them wide and zeroing in on Lea.

Every time I see her, I'm always surprised. She keeps me on my toes. She smiles when I need her to, even though she could never know that I needed her to. I like the way she looks when she's thinking. I like the way she looks at me when I'm thinking.

She talks to squirrels like they're her friends. I think that says a lot about a person, the way they treat animals. It tells you how they'll treat you when you're not saying a word. That they'll talk to you even if you don't say much in return.

It's over so fast I barely have time to notice whether or not he's using adjectives and quite frankly it doesn't really matter. He's so earnest with his feelings that there's no way I could ever give him less than an A. And he did do a good job describing Lea.

I turn to look at her and she is, of course, sitting there red faced and smiling, squirming slightly in her seat. He doesn't look at her, just drops his printout on my desk and takes his seat in the back.

"Thanks, Gabe," I say. He nods and looks like he's in the throes of panic.

"So, who would like to follow up that great example?"

"Isn't 'surprised' an adjective?" Hillary says.

"Shut up, Hillary," Lea mutters, taking the words out of my mouth. "I'll go next."

Hillary sits there, stunned and silent, mouth hanging open as Lea gets up to read.

"Not to be outdone by Gabe," she says, catching his attention, "here's my description, also exactly a hundred words."

"Excellent." I make a "go ahead" gesture. I can still feel Hillary fuming somewhere behind me, but I give Lea my full attention.

He stands like he doesn't want anyone to look at him. I look anyway because I want to, because his posture forces me to. If he didn't want me to look, he'd have to stop existing altogether. Because I never know when he might look back. I want to make sure I'm prepared.

If I miss my moment, I may never get another chance. And if I don't get another chance, he'll never know that I was looking in the first place. Because that's the kind of person he is, the kind of person that makes you want to look.

I can't wait to tell Pam that they both took the bait, and they ran with it. I am so impressed with both of them. I give Lea a thumbs-up as she hands me her paper and then takes her seat.

I take a second to turn and look at Gabe. He's hunched over at his desk, his arms crossed, hugging himself, but his expression is priceless. His smile looks like it's ready to explode off his face and he keeps blinking and shaking his head.

"All right, so far, so good. Let's keep moving!" I say.

Bench *(on the green)*

Why is it that as soon as the days get warmer, I have to take part in every personal conversation on Earth? Don't these kids ever talk in private?

As soon as this ass took a seat, I knew I was in for it. Even if it's my favorite rear end, the best butt I've ever known, I can tell by the way he's sitting that he's waiting for someone.

"Hi," a female voice says.

"Hi," the butt owner says.

They're quiet for a long minute.

"Can I sit?" the girl asks.

"Of course." Nobody ever asks *me* if they can sit.

"So . . ."

"I liked your essay."

"I liked yours, too."

More silence.

"I'm so sorry about the other night," the girl says. "It's all I can think about and I was trying to come up with some better way to say it. And if I didn't think it would be completely humiliating I would have stood in front of the class and said it. But then I started thinking about Hillary listening and judging. I just . . ."

"Hey, it's okay," he says. "I'm sorry, too."

"I'm sorry I was stupid."

"No way. I was way more stupid."

"Maybe we should both try to be less stupid. I hereby pledge to make you act less stupid," she says, holding her hand up like she's taking an oath.

"For the record, I'll still probably be pretty stupid some-times. I make no promises that you'll have the positive influence on me that you assume you'll have."

"You know I don't really think you're stupid."

"Well, how about this," he says, pausing for a long moment. "A compromise. Sometimes I act stupid."

"Of course. But everyone acts stupid sometimes. You don't think I was being stupid when I basically attacked you about talking to Hillary?"

"I don't know, I thought it was kind of cute."

"You say that now, but I promise you, it was stupid."

"This conversation is kind of stupid."

"A little bit, yeah."

"I think we're overusing the word 'stupid.' We'll have to put that on the no-no list along with 'stuff.'"

She laughs. "We are, but that's okay. Nothing wrong with pointless conversation sometimes. It's like . . . practice."

"Why, do we have some kind of big conversational exam coming up?"

She shifts to sit up straighter and he mirrors her movement. I think they must look at each other for a long time. At least I have a few minutes of peace and quiet.

"Stop looking at my ear," he says.

"I'm not looking at your ear."

"Yes, you are."

"Well, now I am," she says, squinting at his ear. "It's totally invisible."

"It's not a big deal, it's really tiny," he says.

"And it helps?" she asks. She shifts closer to him, like she was just waiting for an excuse to enter his personal bubble.

He inches toward her, too, until their legs are touching. "The doctor wasn't sure if this kind would work for me, but I guess I lucked out."

"It seems like maybe you did." Her voice is so soft now, I'm not sure I'd be able to hear her if they weren't sitting right here. "I like you. You know that, right?"

"Yeah. The essay helped me figure that out."

"That's what I was hoping."

"Me too, I mean, I like you, too."

"Do you have anywhere you need to be right now?"

"Nowhere."

They sag into each other and I can tell I'm going to be stuck with them for a while.

I suppose there are worse couples to have to listen to.

———————

Maxine (a waitress)

When they walk in, I can immediately tell something is different. Everything about them is less tense, like all of the anxiety has washed out of them. Not to mention the fact that they're actually coming in together, at the same time, and he's holding the door for her, like the good fella I knew he could be.

"Pick a seat," I tell them. It's quiet; the semester is almost over and one of the young girls called in sick tonight, so I'm hostessing and waitressing. I don't mind a bit, particularly if it means I get to see my favorite couple.

"How are you?" she asks, turning toward me.

"Well, I'm peachy," I tell her. "How are you two tonight?"

"I don't know about Gabe, but I'm starving," she says.

"Me too," he agrees.

"What have you two been up to today?" I ask. I'm feeling nosy.

"We took the train into the city and walked around mostly," he says.

"It was sort of perfect," she says.

"Sounds like you had a good time," I say.

They nod and smile.

"Do you all need another minute or two to decide?"

"Yes, please," she says.

"Let me know when you're ready."

I go behind the counter and start filling saltshakers, making sure to stay within earshot because there's something about these two that I can't get enough of.

"Hey, Lea," the boy says.

"Mmm? I can't decide between grilled cheese and an omelet."

"Look up for a second," he says.

She does.

"I've been meaning to do this all day." He leans across the table and plants her one right on the lips and then pulls back after a few seconds.

"That was a good idea," she says.

Oh, these two sweethearts are going to be the end of me.

Squirrel!

The boy and the girl are back and actually together. I race toward them, ready to throw myself at their feet for whatever delicious treat they've brought me this time.

They're sitting on my favorite bench and his arm is around her and their heads are close and they're talking.

"So, you want to know the basics," she says, twining their hands together.

"Yeah, I feel like I don't know much about you. I know lots of tidbits, but very few facts. Stuff like parents, siblings, birthday, favorite ice cream flavor?"

"Not very interesting. Divorced parents, I mostly see my dad because my mom's remarried with two kids of her own that she's raising more attentively than she ever did with me." She pauses. "Not that I'm super bitter about it or anything."

"Sucks," he says. I like how he's twirling her hair around his finger. I wish someone would twirl my tail like that.

She shrugs. "I'm getting over it."

"How do you get over something like that?"

"This conversation might be more like fourth-date material," she says. "So I'm going to move on to the rest of those questions. Birthday, June fourth."

"Coming up soon," he says. "Let me add that to the old calendar."

"Favorite ice cream flavor would have to be mint chocolate chip."

"I will buy you a tub of it for your birthday. . . ."

She giggles and leans in closer to him.

I decide not to bother them. I have plenty to eat.

Frank (Chinese-food delivery guy)

Only a couple of nights until the end of the school year and I'm delivering out to the freshman dorms again. I should be at home studying for my physics final, but I could really use the money. Maybe I should get someone to read me my notes while I drive.

When I bring the order up to the door, the guy and girl I always assume are dating are actually sitting outside.

"That's for us," the girl says.

"Hey, you finally took my advice and ordered together!"

They laugh.

"I was hoping that would happen."

"You're not the only one," the boy says.

They give me an awesome tip.

Danny (Lea's friend)

I am storming Lea's dorm room in the name of what the hell is going on with her and Gabe. I haven't heard from her since Starbucks last week and I need to get the update. I can barely concentrate on studying for finals.

I come down the hallway and her door is just barely ajar. Excellent, that means she's probably in there and I can corner her and get the information I'm looking for.

I push the door open wide.

"Azalea Fong," I say, putting on my most serious voice.

Then I notice the litter of Chinese food containers across the dresser. And the TV playing an episode of what I think is *Buffy the Vampire Slayer*.

Oh dear, and there are two people tangled up in each

other in a nest of pillows on the floor.

I cover my eyes and yelp as I turn to leave.

"Danny?" Lea gasps, sitting up.

Gabe sits up, too.

Luckily they're both fully clothed.

"I am so sorry," I say.

"It's okay," Lea says, standing up. Gabe follows suit, although he stands a little behind her and doesn't quite meet my eyes. She takes his arm and pulls him in front of her.

"Gabe, this is Danny."

I lean over to shake his hand.

"Nice to meet you," Gabe says.

"We've actually met once or twice. You lived on the same floor with my housemate Maureen."

"Did you used to have blond hair?" Gabe asks, examining my face.

"It was a phase."

"Oh, yeah! I asked about your jeans once because my mom's always bugging me about what brand jeans I want. And I kind of don't care about brands. But she does, I guess."

Everything makes a lot more sense now.

"Well, I'll let you two get back to your date."

"Thanks, Danny," Lea says, reaching to give me a hug. "We'll talk soon, I promise."

"Pinky promise?"

She rolls her eyes, but hooks her pinky to mine.

I close the door behind me as I leave, so no more stragglers interrupt them.

Well, that was mortifying.

But my God, they're adorable.

Acknowledgments

I have a feeling this might get slightly out of hand, so let's start at the very beginning with Jean Feiwel. Without her brilliant idea to mix young adult books and *The X Factor*, this wouldn't be happening. I appreciate everything that she's done for me.

A bucket of gratitude to my editor, Holly West, whose help and patience through the editing process has been nothing short of amazing. This novel would only be half as good without her insights. Also thanks to Molly Brouillette, Allison Verost, and Kathryn Little for a variety of things along the way. And to the Swoon Reads community for all of their reading, rating, and reviewing.

Boatloads of appreciation to my friends and coworkers at the Morristown and Morris Township Library for their flexibility and support: Maria Norton, Chad Leinaweaver, Arlene Sprague, Kelly Simms, Virginia Lee, and Anne Ryan Dello Russo, in particular. Also Jim Collins, for listening to every outrageous book idea I've had during the past four years. Someday, I'm going to write that zombie-mermaid saga.

Endless thanks to the online contingent: Kandra Rivers for

her draft reading and encouragement to keep going, Hanna Nowinski for not blocking my e-mail address after the 5,000th message I sent about trying to find the perfect "aw" moment, and Adi Lubotzki for having a thoroughly intriguing answer to the question "What kind of romance novel do you want to read?" And to all my Tumblr friends and followers, you gave me the *courage* to post my writing in the first place.

Eternally indebted to Lauren Velella, because every time I say, "Hey, I wrote some junk, you wanna read it?" she answers, "Always!" To Michelle Petrasek for being a dynamite reader, editor, gambling buddy, and IHOP enthusiast. To Chrissy George for being my first beta and favorite person to shop with. And a quick shout-out to the FRLK girls—Kate Vasilik, Katie Nellen, Chelsea Reichert, and Melanie Moffitt—for listening and for making me cry using only a call number and an ISBN.

Major props and nothing but love to my sister and brothers: Karen, Scott, and Sean, because a little bit of you leaks into everything I write. You have far more influence on me than you could imagine. Also thanks to Bill, Billy, Zak, Sandra, Brianna, and Kathleen for being a part of this big old family.

Forever grateful to my mom, Pat, for a million reasons, far too many to enumerate here. I would also like to apologize for the foul language. Finally, to my dad, Wayne, whom I miss every day. I like to imagine when he found out this news, he would have said something along the lines of "Way to be, Sandra Jean!" and then bought me a cake.

Turn the page for some

Swoonworthy

Extras....

A Coffee Date

with author Sandy Hall and her editor, Holly West

"About the Author"

Holly West (HW): Do you have a favorite fictional couple? Who is your OTP?

Sandy Hall (SH): My One True Pairing, forever, is Kurt and Blaine from *Glee*. Always, yes.

HW: What's your favorite way to spend a rainy day?

SW: This is so dorky, and I know I'm probably supposed to say something like "reading, curled up," but I love to clean. I hate cleaning any other time, but if it's raining and I'm not going anywhere, I'm going to clean.

HW: Do you have any hobbies that you're really into?

SH: Just reading.

HW: Reading takes up so much time.

SH: It does! It takes up a lot of time, and then you know, watching TV takes up a lot of time . . . being in fandom, stuff like that. It's busy, busy work.

HW: It really is. But you can't write properly if you don't know what's going on.

SH: No, you need to be up on things. Pop culture, the news, you never know where your next inspiration's going to come from.

"The Swoon Reads Experience"

HW: How did you learn about Swoon Reads?
SH: I saw a Huffington Post article linked on Tumblr about it. I read it and thought "This is interesting. I should tell the kids about this at work." Because the librarian always kicks in, and then I thought, "No, I am going to write a book for them. And I'm not going to tell anyone about it because I don't want the kids to read it. Yet."

HW: I love that the first manuscript we chose was one written specifically for our site.
SH: Obviously, I talk to a lot of teens, and I figured I would see what a teen wanted to read, so I wrote an e-mail to one of my online friends that lives in Israel. She's 18, and I said, "Adi, what kind of romance novel do you want to read?" And she came back with this gigantic paragraph, "And they live side-by-side, and they go to the same restaurant, and they . . ." At first, I was like, "Alright, alright . . ." Then I said, "Wait. And then I tell it from everyone else's point of view." It's just a real simple romance, from everybody else's point of view.

HW: What was it like being part of the Swoon Reads site?
SH: I loved reading everyone's comments and feedback. Not only on mine, but on everyone's. November and December are very busy for me professionally, so I didn't have a lot of time to read each and

every manuscript, but I feel like I got a really good taste of them by reading other people's comments. And there was a lot of great writing advice like, "Oh you know, as I read this, I was thinking. . . ." It's just a really nice community, and a lot of serious writers.

HW: So, once you were chosen, you had that great story that you told us about your mom...?
SH: Oh, my mom! So, it was a snow day and I was home, so I told my mom and she said, "Sandra, if they're asking you for $15,000, you should not give it to them." And I had to explain, "No, Mom, Mom, it's a real thing, it's Macmillan, this is the advance." She replied, "It's a scam, be careful!" And I was like, "Mom, Macmillan." Finally, she says, "Oh right, yes. I've heard of them." So, she's always on the lookout for scams apparently. She worries about these things.

HW: It's her job. She is your mother.

"About the Book"

HW: The version that was published is very different from the one originally posted on the site. What in your opinion was the biggest change, and which one was the hardest?
SH: I think the biggest and the hardest are the same—making Lea younger was really hard for me. I think in part because I wrote them both as juniors because I LOVED my junior year of college, like I just had so much fun my junior year. And then to take her back to being a freshman was hard because I had to, you know, make her

a little more naïve and a fish out of water. And I really did like that stuff, but it was hard because I was like, "I know what you will be in two years. You have such potential Lea, I love you! You're going to be okay, we'll just make you young."

HW: Just because this always amazes me, exactly how long did it take you to write this book?
SH: It took me six days.

HW: Which is the shortest answer I have ever heard.
SH: I planned for weeks, the planning started early October, with all of my index cards and spreadsheets and yada yada. And I had dialogue planned out, I had a lot of stuff to grow from, and I had a long weekend—I had a Thursday to a Tuesday off, and I just wrote the heck out of everything. There were days when I wrote like, 12,000 words. It just flowed. I think it was the format of the book, writing from all of those different perspectives. I didn't have to get mired down in anything. The plot just kind of kept moving along, and when something wasn't working, I could just say, "Next!"

HW: Okay, this is your chance to tell me what a terrible person I am. What was it like getting the edit letter?
SH: Oh my God, no. It was amazing! It was like terrifying, and then I read it and I said, "What was I afraid of?" And you were so apologetic, and I was like, "About what?" For starters, I wrote this thing in six days, and then I put it on the Internet for people to read—of course, there's going to be stuff that needs to get changed!

Swoon Reads

HW: I didn't know that. There were some big changes—including going from 23 viewpoints down to only 14, which was going to require you to basically rewrite half the book—and I didn't want to inadvertently crush your soul.

SH: I promise my soul was not crushed. My index cards totally saved the day here. In the first draft, I had an index card for each scene. And they were all color coded. Scenes with Gabe and Lea were white cards, just Gabe was yellow, just Lea was pink, and if neither of them were in the scene the card was orange. Green cards marked the months. So basically I went through and looked at the cards that were for the POVs we were eliminating and I thought about who could sort of take over those moments and then pretty much just made a new card. I ended up making a whole new stack of cards because I needed to switch some other scenes and POVs around, but the index card system really lends itself to edits. It was definitely a major help.

HW: Right, and after that it was just giant outlines—I feel like your writing style and my editing style line up really closely.

SH: Yes, it was really, really easy in that respect. And like I said, wrapping my head around making Lea younger was the hardest part, and once I got over that—oh, and once I added Sam.

HW: Sam is awesome!

SH: Yeah, making Gabe a little younger, I needed to give him another connection. This way, his friends are his brother's friends, and everybody's sort of a group as opposed to Gabe being a loner. Sam really brings him into everything. And I really love Sam—he was my eureka moment. I was sitting at work, totally normal, and all of a sudden, I was like, "He has a brother!"

HW: Brilliant. And I love Sam's voice, too. He's just such a great older brother and I keep having visions of him putting his hand right in the middle of Gabe's back and pushing him forward, saying, "Talk to her!" Just shoving.

SH: Which is basically what he's always wanted to do. It's funny, you know. I think Sam's always wanted to do that, but I don't think Gabe ever really liked a girl as much as he likes Lea. I mean, yeah, he liked girls—but before Lea, it was sort of like, "Eh, I don't think I really want to put myself out there enough to even say that I like this girl."

"The Writing Life"

HW: When did you realize you wanted to be a writer?

SH: Like last summer. I feel like such a jerk sometimes, talking about this, but I think it always kind of was in the back of my head. I kept a journal as a kid, but it was usually just, "Today, I talked to that boy" or "Mom is being mean." I never really wrote anything creatively. I joined Fandom and I wrote some fan fiction, and I realized, "I really love to write. I had no idea I love to write. I failed writing in college. I can't believe how much I love to write!" So, I feel like I have a lot of novels in me now, it's kind of amazing.

HW: Do you have any writing rituals?

SH: I actually have a great writing ritual I have to tell you about. Sometimes when I'm a little bit blocked and I don't know what I'm doing, I just need to settle down and get writing. So, I'll lay out ten wintergreen Life Savers, the individually wrapped ones, or jelly beans or Skittles or whatever. And I can only have one after I've written a certain number of words. And it works. The next thing I know, I have 2,000 words because I just really wanted the candy.

HW: That's great, and it's such a little thing. Let's talk a little bit about your process. Some people just kind of make it up as they go, some people do outlines. What about you?
SH: I do everything. I plan, down to the nitty-gritty. I love my index cards, I love spreadsheets, I dabble with the snowflake method.

HW: What is the snowflake method?
SH: That is where you start off with a sentence, and then you grow that to five sentences. And then you take those five sentences and you grow them to five paragraphs. And then you work on your characters a little bit, and start incorporating them together until it grows and grows and gets more detailed, like a snowflake.

And that's what I put into the spreadsheet, one scene on each line of the spreadsheet. People often tell me, "Spreadsheets don't go with writing," and I'm like, "You don't understand!" I like having a projected word count for a scene and trying to hit that. I don't know! I just really like spreadsheets. And index cards!

HW: I loved looking at your index cards.
SH: They're like my security object now. Like, "Look, I turned these into a book!"

HW: One last question. What is the best writing advice that you've ever heard?

SH: I love Chuck Wendig's blog Terrible Minds, and I was reading a post from a guest writer named Delilah Dawson, who has a very funny little take on "You just have to get it out there." Just write the thing. Stop worrying about it, stop thinking about what it should be or it should look like, and just write it.

And from that moment on, I felt, "I know how to write this. I just need to stop self-editing and thinking, and just write it." And I think that's why, with Gabe and Lea, I wrote it so fast. I had no choice, because if I stop, I start to second-guess myself. I have to get it out. If I stop and think about it for too long, nothing is going to happen.

a Little Something Different

Discussion Questions

1. Did you enjoy the multiple points of view? Would this story have worked as well if it had been told in a more traditional format?

2. What are your feelings about Gabe and Lea? Do you think you would have seen them differently if you had been inside their heads?

3. Which scenes from the book would you have liked to have read from Gabe's point of view? Which scenes from Lea's?

4. Which character had your favorite point of view? Which was your least favorite?

5. Why do you think extremely untraditional viewpoints like the bench and the squirrel were included?

6. Do you feel that all of the narrators were reliable, or did their various personal filters change the way you saw different events?

7. At one point, Gabe makes a list of things he should have said to Lea, but didn't. One of them was "And there's a lot of stuff I should tell you, because you might not like me as much if you know the other stuff, but maybe you still would." Why do you think he believes that? Has there been any indication on Lea's

part that she might not like him if she really got to know him?

8. What do you think of Inga's creative writing assignments? Would you be able to write a description of someone without using adjectives?

9. Have you ever been in this situation of watching two people try to fall in love? If you were friends with Gabe and Lea, what advice would you have given them?

10. If you could pick any of the characters in this novel to have their own story, which would you choose?

Want to host your own
Swoon Reads Book Club Party?
Download our *free* event kit at
www.swoonreads.com/partykit!

© Susana Ramirez

Sandy Hall is a teen librarian from New Jersey, where she was born and raised. She has a BA in Communication and a Master of Library and Information Science from Rutgers University. When she isn't writing or teen librarian-ing, she enjoys reading, marathoning TV shows, and long scrolls through Tumblr. *A Little Something Different* is her first novel.

A tale of fanfiction,
family and first love

FANGIRL

Cath and Wren are identical twins and until recently they did
absolutely everything together. Now they're off to university
and Wren's decided she doesn't want to be one half of a pair
any more – she wants to dance, meet boys, go to parties and
let loose. It's not so easy for Cath. She would rather bury
herself in the fanfiction she writes where there's romance far
more intense than anything she's experienced in real life.

Now Cath has to decide whether she's ready to open
her heart to new people and new experiences,
and she's realizing that there's more to learn
about love than she ever thought possible . . .

RAINBOW ROWELL

Twelve Winter Romances

MY TRUE LOVE
GAVE TO ME

Holly Black ✳ Ally Carter ✳ Matt de la Peña
Gayle Forman ✳ Jenny Han
David Levithan ✳ Kelly Link
Myra McEntire ✳ Stephanie Perkins
Rainbow Rowell ✳ Laini Taylor ✳ Kiersten White

Edited by Stephanie Perkins

REBECCA SERLE

FAMOUS
IN LOVE

I'll tell you what it's like to
be with him. How he kisses
me. How he touches my
cheek. How he holds my pinkie,
just slightly, so the cameras won't
catch us touching.

When seventeen-year-old Paige Townsen gets plucked
from obscurity to star in the movie adaptation of a
blockbuster book series, her life changes practically
overnight. Within a month, Paige has traded the quiet
streets of her hometown for a bustling movie set
on the shores of Maui, and she is spending
quality time with her costar Rainer Devon,
one of *People*'s Sexiest Men Alive.